When the
Sparrow Sings

a novel

by Jason Linden

When the Sparrow Sings
A FanGraphs/The Hardball Times production

Edited by Joe Distelheim and Paul Swydan
Illustrations by Brooke Howell
Cover design by Travis Howell
Typesetting by Paul Swydan

ISBN-13: 978-1503398658
ISBN-10: 150339865X
Printed by CreateSpace

For Cate

"Oh, Jake," said Brett, "we could have had such a damned good time together."

- Ernest Hemingway,
The Sun Also Rises

Pregame.

"I am going to pitch." This is the first thing I say and the only thing that matters. Cameras snap and reporters ask questions. I don't know what I am supposed to say or do. Am I supposed to smile or not? I try to look quietly dignified. Someone asks a question and I miss it completely.

I shouldn't be up here.

"Um, listen guys, I appreciate that you all have questions, but I'm going to turn it over to Cam and Jerry here. I just thought it was important that I be here for the announcement. I mean, that I make the announcement."

Maybe this was a mistake. Why did they ask me to do a press conference? Couldn't they just send out a press release? They could just tweet it for all I care. They wanted me up here. Cameron said it would help team morale. I don't know why. Now I just have to not look too sad. I think that's my job. I'll try to be attentive. Jerry is talking. What do you have to say, skip?

"Right now, we have Zack scheduled to start game two. I said that yesterday, and I don't see any reason to change. He's had a shock, we all know that, and we want to let him recover."

Right, Jerry, right. My dad died. That's why you're holding me until game two of the Series. It's not, I don't know, that I'd be going on short rest in game one and you can only have me for two games anyway. Good framing there. I can tell you used to catch. The reporters are eating it up. They're scribbling away. The better ones will point out that game two means regular rest for me. The lazy ones will just take what he's feeding them.

Christ. Just get me out of here.

* * *

The World Series starts in a few hours. I am staring at my phone. I have been staring at my phone all day. I can do that right now and no one will blame me. If it weren't for the situation, I'd be aloof. Maybe even a clubhouse cancer if I stared at my phone while frowning. But now, it's just grief. No one wants to talk to me anyway.

Let's see what the headlines are after the little press conference.

Hiatt: "I'll Pitch."

Short, but sweet, I like it.

Fan Reaction: Our Hero

That's a little over the top, isn't it? What if I didn't pitch? What if I stink? I really might stink. Will I be a villain then? Yes, though no one will say it. You can't just blast someone for having a bad day at work when his father dies. You can think it though. And some people would say it. You know they would. I'd walk down the street, pass some goon and hear my manhood questioned. None of the articles will say that, will they? *We Made Him Do It* or *Hiatt MUST Pitch.* It writes itself.

October 18th –

In the wake of a father's tragic death in a car accident the day after watching his son pitch his team into the World Series, the son, star pitcher Zack Hiatt made the announcement required of him by our absurd, sports-obsessed culture.

"I'm obviously very broken up," said Hiatt, "but I know in this society, there is almost nothing more important than winning a championship in sports. Obviously, my grief over my father's death must take a backseat to the requirements of the public in this matter. Otherwise, I would spend the rest of my life regarded as a spineless pariah."

It's impossible to deny the wisdom in what Hiatt says. Despite the supposed outpouring of understand-

ing over his tragic loss, it is undeniable that all those concerned—media, fans, and team management—saw Hiatt's predicament as having only one solution. Indeed, it can be seen clearly in quotes from around the baseball world:

A Fan:

"Obviously, I understand how broken up he must be. I'm really close to my dad, and I'd be a wreck if he died. But, you know, it's been a long time since we had a championship in this city and Hiatt has been a huge part of this team. I don't know if they can do it without him."

From General Manager Cameron Bunton:

"I've spoken to Zack, and he knows he'll have whatever he needs from us. He's been absolutely vital to this team and, though we're obviously better with him, we do believe we have a shot even if he decides he isn't ready to go."

In the light of such clear statements regarding the priorities of those who control his professional destiny, there is no doubt that Hiatt must pitch. Indeed, he must perform well to avoid being seen as lacking the capacity to compete in the face of adversity. Players who earn the reputation of being "soft" find that it dogs them for the rest of their careers.

Sigh. I don't really know that that's true, I guess, but it feels true. I shouldn't have looked at the comments. Why can't we all learn to never read the comments? Yes, I am rich. I am hugely, unbelievably rich. When I was small my dad worked in a factory and my mom was a bookkeeper and we were always got by, but now that almost seems like poverty. At least it does when I don't have any perspective. I am rich. But what does that mean? How much money do I have to give up to be allowed to be a person? If I were like my parents, no one would doubt. No one would question. *Sure Zack, take a couple of weeks off. Go be with your family. It's hard losing a parent like that.* I'm not like them, though.

At least there's a baseball game today. Pitch charting and mental preparation. Maybe that will help.

* * *

This is not going to feel right. There is no right. It feels wrong to pitch. They are burying my dad tomorrow. They put off the funeral for me. Because I can't get off work.

Oh Jesus. I should not start crying before I pitch in the World Series. That would be bad. Especially with reporters crawling everywhere. No, I should not start crying.

But it would feel wrong not to pitch, too. It's the World Series. And then there's dad. It's not like I went into this against his wishes. He might have wanted this more than me. He absolutely wanted this more than me. I am aware that it might never happen again. This may be the only chance I ever have to pitch in the World Series. And if I don't go, they're stuck with Sharp, who's a nice guy, but he doesn't belong on a playoff roster.

I wonder. If someone had taken me onto the field last night after we lost and the place had emptied so quickly and the only people left were those cleaning the stands. If they had stood me there on the mound. Or maybe not on the mound, but on the edge of the grass behind third base. If they had let me look at the destroyed baselines and the nonexistent batter's boxes and the spot over behind short where Manny slipped and took up the turf, but still made the catch. If they had stood me there and said, "It is your choice. No one will hate you if you say no and no one will love you if you say yes. The lights will be bright like this, but the lines will be clean and the turf will be patched and the stands will be full and it will be your game and it will be what you always wanted it to be. And the timing will be wrong and it will feel wrong. But it will be yours and there are no consequences beyond that choice. Beyond what you feel." If they had done that and then walked off the field and left me standing there as long as I wanted before I had to decide. What would I have said?

I don't know.

But no one did that. No one has asked me how I felt or what I wanted. It has been assumed that my grief is simple. Two-dimensional. Either my father's death is too much for me or it is not. Either I have the stones to soldier through it—if we want to get into baseball cliché—or I do not.

Can it be both? That feels the most right. It is too much and I must pitch. But if dad knew—if he knew that I did not pitch and that it was because of him. What would he say to that? He only ever talked about my career in the plural. We've worked for this your whole life, Zack. This is our dream. This is what it's all about. We finally get to see what you can do on the big stage. Only on that last night before the accident was it different. Would it dishonor his memory? Or would it say something else? Would it say that he mattered beyond baseball even if he only ever thought in baseball?

"What? No, no. Tell him I can't talk now. I'm getting ready."

"You know what they're going to think, right?" This is John, our hitting coach.

"Yeah, I know. How could I not know? Do you think I'm stupid!

"Wait, wait, come back, John. I'm sorry man. They're right to think that, you know. I know you guys, all the coaches and the players, too, you don't want to think that and you don't want anyone else to think that, but it's true. I'm sorry I yelled. It doesn't matter anyway. I'm pitching. Now, it only matters how I pitch. I'll talk after. Tell them I'll talk after the game. Tell them I'm gathering my thoughts. That will sound better. It'll give them something they can put on the blog or in the paper or on Twitter. That's all they want."

I love John. I think it might be weird for a pitcher to be so close with the hitting coach—I don't even get to pretend to hit like NL pitchers—but I am. We went to the same college. Well, he went. I visited for a couple of years. We even had the same coach. He's good at seeing weak spots in hitters, but we don't really talk about that. John's a smart guy. He only ever got to Triple-A, but he has a real college degree. He double majored in literature and biology and he was the starting third baseman for four years. That's amazing. He gives me books to read. I told him how I think too much between starts and he started giving me stuff to read. So we talk about that mostly.

I'm glad he's going to be back next year. Last year, the guys didn't hit as well as everyone thought they should and there was talk about maybe letting him go. Almost everybody hit this year. There's no way he's not coming back with how our offense was.

I have ninety minutes. For ninety minutes I will be a hero. The fans do not care if I talk to the media. The tragedy, they think, has given me the choice of not talking. For ninety minutes, they will love me, and then I will take the mound and I will pitch. If I pitch well, everyone—the fans, the reporters, my teammates—will believe I used this time to gather strength. If I pitch poorly, they will believe I was falling apart. That I never should have been allowed to pitch. It is cold to think this, but how I pitch today will affect how much money teams are willing to pay me when this is over. It will affect whether or not this team wants to re-sign me. If

I pitch well, I am a superstar. If I do not, I am a question mark with make-up issues. These are the clichés we use to try and glean the truth.

But for ninety minutes they will cheer me because they do not want my life right now. When I step on the mound, it will be deafening. I have that. I have ninety minutes, and then we will see. Time to get ready.

* * *

"How's your arm today?"

"Good. It's good, Petey." That's a smart question. These bullpen catchers are always good for that kind of thing. They know how to keep the mood up. That's how they keep their jobs. They don't have the skills to play, but they can stick around forever if they make pitchers feel comfortable. Petey wants to know about my arm. He doesn't want to know about my head and he doesn't want me to think about my head. The arm. Let's focus on the arm. Fastballs first.

"Good, that's good. Don't turn it up too high yet. Still getting warm."

Popped it too hard. That was probably ninety-five. He's right. Too early for that. Fastballs. Not one-hundred percent. Take it down.

"That's good. That's better. Ease into it. Game hasn't started yet. Don't get too excited."

Yes, the game. The game. Only the game. I see Dave watching me over there. He's staying quiet, but I see him. He wants to know where my head is. John will have told him about my outburst. He's thinking of what he'll say if he has to come out to the mound later. If I give up a homer or, worse, if I can't get the ball over. That's what I have to worry about. That's what he's worried about. If I think too much, I lose control. That's always been my problem. Or it was. I figured it out. Don't think. Just pitch. *Bull Durham*. Here comes Dave.

"Okay, you're lookin' good. A little strong maybe, but it's a big game, so that's okay. Better to get it out now. Let's get Brian in here, work the off-speed stuff in a little and see where we stand."

"Fastball First."

He told me to get it out. Let's get it out.

"Good, good. Strong arm tonight. Let's see the change."

I heard you suck air, Dave. I heard it. You were afraid that was gonna hit the wall and it did. It's cold. Hard to grip. "Don't worry, ball's slick. Let me give it another run." There we go.

"Okay, slider."

Dirt. Dirt. Ahhh, that didn't even go fifty feet. "Sorry, Brian."

"Hey man, it's fine. Do it now. Don't do it out there." He nods toward the field like we're not already out here. Like cameras aren't watching me now.

Somewhere, there is a seat my dad would have sat in and someone else is there. We all know this, but we're not talking about it. Normal jitters. That's all it is, right? Normal jitters. Just get it out now.

"Let's go again."

Better. Low, but it got there.

"Okay, boys, huddle up. Change looks good. Fastball looks great. Let's stick with those until the jitters are out, then you can start calling the splitter, Brian. Let's start that out with the last couple of guys. Don't want to make a mistake against the middle of that lineup."

Brian and I are both nodding. This is a rational plan. It is just jitters. Normal nerves. The anthem is starting.

* * *

We are in the dugout. In a moment, I will jog out. They will see me. I will hear cheers. They will be loud. I am jogging. They are loud. I know what I am going to do. My cleats grip the turf and pull at the grass. I am jogging onto the field and there is the infield dirt. And they are still screaming. Brian is talking to me, but I cannot hear him. They are screaming and screaming and they love me and these are maybe the last minutes of that. And it is so loud. And here is the mound. A fresh ball. Waxy and cold. Brian is squatting behind the plate. I am rubbing the ball to warm it. Kneading it in my hands. I will throw eight pitches and the game will begin.

I position myself on the rubber. I come set and it is cold and my breath fogs the air in front of me. I cannot smell anything other than the cold. I do not smell the dirt or the grass. It is loud. It is still so loud. I throw. It is clean and true and there are seven pitches left.

Brian throws the ball back. The sound as it hits my glove is more crack than pop because it is cold and the leather is stiff instead of supple. I use the toe of my cleat to dig away at the dirt in front of the rubber. This is the thirty-seventh time I have stood on the mound before the start of a game this year and each time the mound has been perfect and each time I have thrown my first warm-up pitch and then dug away with my cleat because it never feels quite perfect. I wonder if this bothers the groundsman who handles the mound. I wonder if sees himself contributing to the beautiful thing that is a field before the game begins and if he sees that the game is also beautiful. Or, perhaps, he sees me as a parasite fouling his work. I don't know. I think it is probably the former, but I always wonder. My hole is dug and I throw the next pitch and it tails a little on me, but Brian reaches it and gloves it and tosses it back and there are six pitches left.

I have been going wrong all day. All day the routine has been off, but now, as I approach my third pitch, and my left foot settles into the hole I have made in front of the rubber, the crowd quiets for just a moment—readying itself for the roar of the first real pitch—and I forget about the cold. It is just like a normal game. It is something I have done before almost two hundred times since I was brought up to stay. The crowd chatters and vendors shout and the world spins. I throw again. This one is true. I hit the spot set for me. It pops in his glove and he throws it quickly back and there are five pitches left.

I feel fine now. I see Juan Ramirez standing off to the side, swinging the bat loosely, feeling the cold as I do, and trying to shake it out. My foot finds its spot against the rubber and everything stays in place. I hit my spot again. Four pitches to go.

The ball comes back to me and snaps into my glove, which is working loose against the heat of my hand. As I settle in, the wind shifts and the smell of fresh hot dogs and popcorn finds its way to me on the mound. Maybe it is my imagination, but I swear I can feel the heat of the concession stand. It breaks through the cold and I lose whatever zone I have been in because I am thinking of dad now and how he always used to buy me a hot dog before the start of a game. "So you don't get hungry later." My dad never drank alcohol at ballgames. He didn't want to have to go to the bathroom. If the day was hot and it was late in the game, he might indulge in a soda. But mostly it was water. The ballpark was his classroom. Even when I was six or seven, I was expected to hold my bladder all the way through. If I insisted, he would take me, but it was never worth it. I always felt it would have been better to go in my pants. I never did, though. I was afraid of his wrath if he decided a cleanup was needed. I am thinking of this and Brian is looking at me and I realize I have been standing without moving for longer than is normal. I shake it off and throw. It bounces just in front of him, but he stops it easily. Tosses it back and says to relax. There are three pitches left.

I see Ramirez off to the side again. He's moved closer so he can time me. He's just a kid. From the Dominican, I think. It's only his second year and I've never faced him before, but I know the scouting report. He might be a very nice kid, but right now, he terrifies me. I see him and I think what my dad taught me to think. He wants to hurt me. He is going to try to hurt me. Not directly, of course. But the indirectness somehow makes it worse. It is not just me. It is the other twenty-four. The thousands around us. And I will try to hurt him back. It is a game of hurt. Mostly mental, sometimes physical. I don't think of this often. I stopped a few years ago. It was a part of the thinking too much. It's front and center now. I begin the wind-up. My hands are behind my head and I see a line drive laced down the right field line. Ramirez is fast and before I can blink already there is a man on third. My hands are back to my chest and it is cold. Why is it so cold? Why are we playing this July game now? There are two pitches left.

I have never in my life thought so much during warm-up pitches. Never. When I was young, I fussed over my mechanics. I'm tall and my arms are long and it was hard to get everything working together. I would focus hard and the harder I focused, the more polarized my results were. When I wasn't thinking, I looked like every wild pitcher you have ever seen. Focused, there were only two options. The pitch would knick the corner for the kind of strike that didn't belong on a high school field or it would sail over the catcher and umpire into the chain-link fence. I wedged balls into it sometimes. I knew I was terrifying, but I didn't want to be. I just wanted to pitch. I am not thinking like that now. I am everywhere. My brain cannot decide if it wants to land on the past or on right now. It flits back and forth like a bee darting from blossom to blossom. I have one pitch left.

Everyone suddenly awakes. The batter waits to be announced. The crowd becomes loud. So loud. I have never experienced loudness like this. I have no context. Is it like the inside of a jet engine or is it like the blast from an atomic bomb or is it only a herd of elephants at full sprint? I don't know. But it is loud. I cannot hear anything else but every so often, voices come through and as I am winding up I hear one and it sounds like my dad. I don't know how it makes me feel, but it grabs me so that everything else falls away and the ball rolls out of my fingers and snaps into Brian's glove right where he wanted it. I can tell from the way he pops up to toss it back that he is happy. He feels better about me after that pitch, and he feels the energy, too. He played last night, but this is also his first World Series and he is excited. In slim moments, I become excited too. But it can never wash over me like I know it is washing over Brian and the others. I am alone. Everyone else has someone here, but my dad is not here and my mom is not here because her husband has just died and my sister is not here because her dad has just died. I am here and I walk behind the mound. I pick up the rosin bag and drop it. I climb the mound. I nod at the plate.

And the umpire shouts, "Play ball!" and I tuck the cold white ball into my glove and I stare down the distance between the mound and home, and Ramirez steps in and takes his stance like a bouncing piston ready to force an explosion and I wait for what I know is coming. Brian puts down the sign. A single finger extends downward. I nod. I straighten. I try to relax my shoulders. I breathe out.

Top of the First.

There is nothing apparently terrible in how it begins. I throw the fastball as called for by Brian. I miss a little too far in and the umpire calls ball. This is not how I want to start, but it's nothing special. It's a 1-0 count. I have had thousands of 1-0 counts. They rarely lead to disaster. But I'm tense and a strike would have relaxed me. A ball only adds to the tension. Again, a finger points down. Again, I throw the fastball. Again, I miss my spot, and there are now two balls and no strikes. You are already filling in the blanks. You know what happens here. I cannot find my spots against Ramirez and he walks on four pitches and suddenly the crowd is quiet.

He doesn't come out, but as Ramirez trots down to first, Brian hollers "relax" out to the mound. "Just one batter." He wants me to stop thinking. I want to stop thinking. Stop thinking. Stop thinking. Stop. Think. Ing. Stop. Stop. Stop. I can't stop. Ramirez is fast and he wants to get in my head. He dances around on first. He's testing me. He knows what happened as well as Brian does, but Brian has my best interests in mind. Ramirez doesn't. And so he dances to get in my head. I throw over once and he slides back. A second time and Alex is just able to dig the ball out of the dirt. I settle in to pitch to the next batter. I should not be worried about this guy at all. He should be batting eighth, but some managers want a guy who can bunt up top. I'm not worried about him. My worry is more general. Directionless. I lose it completely and the first pitch sails over Brian and over the umpire and Ramirez dances down to second. It's a thing of beauty, it really is. I love watching those guys who are so thin they almost vanish when they run. It looks so easy. Nothing should look that easy. You blink and they're halfway around the bases. But I can't appreciate it right now. I am much too busy walking the second batter on four pitches. Fortunately, Brian is able to glove the remaining three—though not without some effort—and so it is only first and second.

But the crowd is silent. I could close my eyes and believe I was alone. There is not even a rumble. Vendors do not call out. This is the World Series and it is also their worst nightmare. They are all silently asking if maybe Jerry needs to get someone up in the pen. We lost yesterday. Why doesn't he have someone getting warm now? This is what they want to know. I understand.

Ramirez, at least, shows no sign of going. Why would he risk letting Brian throw him out? I look like I'm going to walk him home any minute.

Brian comes out to the mound.

"Are you okay out here?"

"I don't know. I'm thinking too much. I need an out. I just need one out."

"Take a little off if you need to. Ferris probably won't hit a home run."

"Comforting, Brian. Very comforting."

He walks back to the mound and the best hitter on the other team—Mike Ferris—comes to the plate. Nothing much to see here. Just thirty-seven homers and an unwillingness to swing at anything that is not a strike. Perfect for someone who, at the moment, cannot find the strike zone with both hands and a flashlight. Brian calls for a fastball and I do as he suggests and take a little off because I know with what he has seen so far, Ferris is not thinking about swinging at all. The ball slips in and I get a strike and the crowd relaxes just a little bit. Perhaps we can wait one batter to get someone up.

I look toward the plate and Brian is calling for a slider. That can't be right. We must have the signals mixed up. I shake him off. He runs through them again. Still slider. I shake him off, again. I can barely get my fastball over, why is he calling for a slider. He comes out to the mound again. He does not cover his mouth or whisper. He barely pauses in his stride. He says to throw what he tells me to throw and walks back to the plate.

Fine. You want a slider. Here is a slider.

And it works. I am irritated enough to not think. It is not a great pitch, but it is unexpected and it is good enough. Ferris swings and tops it and it goes right to Manny at short and Manny is sure as hell not going to screw up this double play. He scoops it up and it goes to second and then to first and just like that there are two outs.

I can relax a little bit now. I can pitch from the windup. I do not have to worry about Ramirez on third if I can get this next batter out. But I cannot relax too much. This is Marcus Martin, the right fielder. He hits almost as well as Ferris. More power, but he swings a little too much. Few of us are perfect as players. Ferris is. Russell on our team, much as I hate to admit it. I might be on my better days, but this isn't one of those. Everyone else has flaws, even the great players like Marcus. I've faced him a lot. Until last year, he played for Tampa. He's a good guy, too. I'd probably root for him if I were at home watching. One of the things I've found about being a player is that I pull for other players now more than teams. Every team has some jerks on it. Some teams, like ours, have players who shouldn't qualify as human. That's just the way it goes.

I settle in and look for the sign. After the slider, I'm feeling a little cocky. Brian calls for a fastball and sets up inside. He doesn't swing, but the ball finds the zone and I have my second called strike of the night. I throw another fastball to the same spot, but I miss over the plate just a little. He takes a big swing and fouls it straight back. That was close. The crowd is coming back to me now. They sense that I am on the verge of getting out of this mess.

Brian wants a slider off the plate. We have the advantage and can waste a pitch trying to get him to chase. I oblige, but it doesn't work and the count is one ball and two strikes. We go back to the fastball and again he fouls it off, but this one is scarier than the last. It is long and loud and if it had been thirty feet to the left, the score would be two to zero. Brian and I both know we won't be so lucky with another fastball. He calls for a change-up, hoping Martin will be out in front and we can go to the dugout with a strikeout.

It doesn't work.

He's out in front, but not enough. He sends a line drive between short and third and the score is one to nothing.

I slap my glove against my leg and I swear, but something good has happened. That was a good at-bat. I made all my pitches. He beat me, but it happens. A few minutes ago, we were having a disaster. Now we are having a baseball game. We are losing, that's true, but at least it's a game.

I settle in and I don't think too much and up comes the third baseman, who is probably a better hitter than the guy I just faced - though more of a jerk—but bats fifth because the manager does not want to stack left-handed hitters together. He also has a nasty platoon split. I've faced him a few times before and he's never done anything against me, and I am not especially concerned. Brian and I make him look terrible. Fastball. Fastball. Slider. Back to the dugout. The crowd is cheering so loud, it feels like they've forgotten that we are losing now. I think they are cheering because they too know this is going to be a game and not a massacre. They can feel, regardless of what happens from here on, that I braved and—at least momentarily—triumphed over adversity. This is a good story. It's the one everyone wants.

Except the other side.

Bottom of the First.

I run off the field and into the dugout and Dave hands me a jacket. Everyone is smiling at me. Manny comes and bumps me playfully from behind. And says not to worry, they will take care of me tonight.

"But no more of that walking. That was too much. You get the ground balls and the strikeouts and we will be fine. We will score runs."

I say that I hope they will score runs.

Manny says, "I will even hit a home run if I have to."

Manny does not hit home runs. Manny doesn't really hit. He plays because of his glove. He had two homers this year.

"First time for everything," I say and he shakes his finger at me. It is a nice moment.

Though he is our leadoff hitter, Adam Reynolds looks nothing like Juan Ramirez strolling to the plate. First, and most obviously, he is an almost sickly pale. It is impossible to understand how someone can have a job that requires him to be outside in the sun nearly every day and yet, after eight months of spring training and the regular season and playoffs, can still be so pale. But he is pale. He is also bulky. Ramirez is thin enough to get lost in a sidewalk crack, but Adam looks like the one who made the crack. He isn't fat, or anything like it. He's just large. He doesn't run, either. Adam stole two bases last year, one when a pitcher actually fell down and the other when the catcher threw the ball into center. He'd have been out by five feet otherwise. The only things he has in common with Ramirez are that he gets on base and plays middle infield.

Adam looks incongruous at second, nothing like the small, scrappy player you expect there. Instead, he's kind of a Cal Ripken type; he always puts himself in the right place and he's quick. On lots of teams he'd play short, but we have Manny and no one is better than Manny at short, not even Ramirez. And anyway, he hits well enough to play the outfield, so it's really a bonus that he doesn't trip over himself out there. On top of it all, Adam takes a lot of walks and so, despite the fact that he does not steal a base unless the pitcher falls down, Adam Reynolds is our leadoff hitter.

I feel intent on Adam as he walks to the plate. I am interested to see how this inning goes. To see if we have any spark. But my mind starts to drift almost right away. I am in a calmer place after getting that last strikeout and when I think about my dad it is the early years before baseball became the whole world and, instead, was only a part of it.

* * *

My sister loves baseball the right way. She loves it the right way because she was born first and, knowing his daughter could never play in the major leagues, my dad did not obsess over her abilities. He did not analyze her early batting stances or her form as they played catch. He taught her about baseball as many fathers teach their children and she loved it because she loved him. I have an early memory that may be imagined—a patched-together idea from family photos—but I believe it is real. I am still small enough to be uncertain in my steps. A diaper forces me into the awkward waddle of a toddler and my sister drags me into the family room of our house—a room that had once been a small garage—and directs me in the construction of a baseball field. There is no outfield to speak of, but four stuffed animals are used to represent the bases. She takes up a toy bat, hands me the ball, and calls to Dad that we are ready. He comes in, laughs, and joins in as the catcher. I cannot run properly, but when I throw, it sails straight into his hands—one of the few times I was able to get a ball past Kristen.

"Hey Zack, that's a nice throw, little boy. Good job."

Even knowing what came later, this memory stays clean. It is everything I like about baseball when I was young. I do not feel that Dad was analyzing me yet. He was smart enough to know that at that age, I was as likely to hit the ceiling fan as a target six inches in front of me. We are playing together, the three of us, and it happened because of baseball.

* * *

The crowd cheers and I look up, but it is one of those truncated baseball cheers that falls quickly to a groan. Adam has hit a line drive, but it has been gobbled up at short by Ramirez. It is starting to feel as though this game is between Ramirez and me, rather than Guillen and me. Guillen is a fine pitcher, but I am better than him seven out of ten times. Ramirez is a worthy opponent. I would feel proud to beat him.

Next, I watch Matt walk to the plate. He plays right and looks like he should spend his time launching balls into the upper deck. But he's a little too short maybe and the balls he hits are a little too straight and turn into only singles and doubles. He's not going to bunt anyone over, but he may well drive them in. I tell myself I am going to pay attention to this at-bat. I am trying to stay in the game, but it doesn't work. I am thinking about the game with the stuffed animals and about my sister.

* * *

I was always jealous of Kristen and I think she was jealous of me and I think that is probably why, for a long time, we weren't as close as we could have been. Each of us had the relationship with Dad that the other one wanted. We've gotten closer over the last few years, but it was hard growing up. Kristen wanted to be a baseball player. That is all she wanted to be. She turned her nose up if anyone even mentioned softball. She would have been fine with the pressure, but Dad saw it only as an indulgence and so he was gentler with her. He knew she'd never be pro, but his love of baseball wasn't just about that. He coached her teams in Little League. He cheered her when she made the high school team not just because we were a small school, but because she was really slick at second and could always put the bat on the ball.

She was the starter when I was a freshman. Even then, I had enough of a fastball to play varsity, but I didn't have the control thing totally mastered, so I didn't pitch much. There were a few times, though, when Kristen and I were on the field at the same time. I remember looking out at Dad in the stands and how happy he was. I think those moments, freshman year, were what made me really commit to baseball. If I could make him that happy, if I could make anyone that happy, why not do it?

The year before that had been hard on Dad. That's when I'd done my adolescent rebellion. There wasn't anything special about it. Dad had been driving pretty hard on baseball for a few years by then. I had started entertaining childish notions about being a big leaguer when I was in third grade and Dad had started me on a travel team as soon as he could. By the end of seventh grade it had gotten really intense—some of that was my own doing—and I needed a break and everything he did was stupid anyway, right? So I started diving into what had been minor interests up until then. I had some friends who played those fantasy card games. Magic and that kind of thing. My mom had always read us fairy tales growing up and I liked them. I had some friends playing the games and they seemed like the more grown-up version of those stories, so I started playing. Dad didn't like it. He really didn't like it.

"Why do you want to go spend all day inside with those nerds pretending to be a wizard or something? It's nice out. Let's go work on your delivery."

This was the kind of mistake Dad made. If he'd said play catch or if he'd volunteered to throw batting practice to me, he might have had me. Instead, it was "work on my delivery." That wasn't fun, it was work, and I was a kid. I didn't like work.

"Why do you have to insult my friends?"

"I'm not trying to insult them, Zack. I'm sure it's a good way for them to spend a Saturday. Most of them look allergic to the sun or something. I'm sure they'll grow up to program computer games about dragons. That's not for you, though."

I responded to this exactly like you would expect. I turned around and left. A few days later I told dad I didn't think I'd play that year.

* * *

I'm getting worked up thinking about this and I just want to dwell on it when Matt grounds weakly to Ramirez and I hear the PA boom, "Now batting, center fielder! Russell! Jennings!" I hate Jennings. I hate him. I do not care that he is our best player. That he will probably win the MVP this year. I've played with people I've disliked before and you get over it. You deal with it, but this is different. A good day is when he goes oh-for-four and we win. I'll take a good day for him and a win over a bad day for him and a loss, but not by much. I don't want to think about all that right now. I'm good and worked up over my dad and I want to get back to that and ignore Russell.

* * *

What was hardest on Dad was that, yeah, he'd been pushing me, but it was at my prompting. I wanted to be a ballplayer. It felt to him like I was breaking a promise.

"What do you mean, you don't think you'll play?"

"I don't want to. It's no fun anymore." Lies. Those were lies, but I was hurting him, and that was the point.

"Not even the travel team?"

"I don't want to play at all."

Dad got really mad. His face turned red and he started to shout. I was almost as big as him by then, but it was really scary all the same. "What about everything we've worked for? What do you think you're going to do now? Spend the summer pretending to cast spells with those losers? Why don't I buy you a skateboard and you can start wearing black clothes. Oh, and maybe you can start smoking. Might as well practice being a loser if that's what you want to be."

I had no idea who Dad was describing. None of my friends smoked or skateboarded, though some of them did wear black. I think he was just mixing up counter-cultures.

Telling my dad I wouldn't play, and then following through on it was probably the meanest thing I've ever done, but it was hard on me, too. I wanted to play. I always liked playing baseball and sometimes I loved it. Dad knew that, I think. This is how I make it okay. Telling myself that he wouldn't have pushed so far if he didn't think I wanted it as much as he did. Sometimes, in the car on the way home from practice, he would gripe about other dads pushing their sons too hard because they had flamed out in high school or whatever. "You have to let the kid guide it. Always remember that, Zack. It's up to you, not me."

I wanted to play in eighth grade, but I didn't want to just play baseball. What about my friends? What about girls? I didn't want to give up girls for baseball. Dad understood my pubescent mind. Sometimes, during that year, when I headed out to the game shop where we all hung out, he'd call after me, "You're never going to get a girlfriend in that place. I've never even seen a girl there." And sometimes, if he was feeling especially mean, he'd add, "Girls love ballplayers, though."

God, he was such a jerk that year. It's been a
long time since I thought about how much of a jerk
he was then.

* * *

There is a very loud roar and I watch a long, long
fly ball go very, very foul. The run would be nice,
but I don't know if I want it that way. As though
it matters. As though I haven't already won games
because of him. As though he hasn't saved me runs
and thus made me more money diving for balls in
center.

* * *

I spent a lot of time in that game shop. A lot. It
was a good place, too. It was really, really nerdy,
but I didn't mind that. I still don't. Being a nerd
is just about how you like something. There's a
little bit of obsession to it. It's why most athletes
are good. But the shop. I liked the shop. Our town
was just big enough to support it. We were lucky.
My dad always talked about it like it was a dingy
little basement, but it was actually really nice. It
was bright and always clean and there were tables
for us to play at and the owner was a really nice
guy who never tried to rip you off. It always had
that great cellophane smell. You could go in there
and feel new. Why is it so hard to feel new when
you are thirteen years old? It should be easy, but
it isn't.

That shop was fun, and it pissed off my dad, so it was perfect. The angrier it made him, the more time I spent there. But it was hard going without baseball for a year, and by the time tryouts for the high school team rolled around, I was ready to go back to it.

That year did us both good. I think. For me, it made baseball into a choice. It's easier to do something when it's up to you. I feel bad saying that it put Dad in his place, but it kind of did. He wasn't blind. I mean, obviously he wasn't blind—I'm starting game two of the World Series after all. Dad knew I had a lot of talent. Middle school kids just don't throw that hard. Knowing that I might throw away that talent hurt him, but it also made him gentler with me. He still pushed, but he didn't shove. Which isn't to say we didn't still fight about it all the time. He just had a better sense for when to walk away.

And that's how we got to high school. And that's how Dad got to see me standing on the mound with Kristen at second behind me. That's a nice memory to rest on. I want to find these good memories and just hold onto them because they don't mess with my head like Dad teasing me about my Magic cards or girls. I like to think of how it was before I even threw a pitch. Just standing on the mound. Or maybe running out with Kristen next to me, bumping into me playfully and telling me not to embarrass myself and hearing Dad yell for us both. And how hot it was because we always played during the day and it was that kind of Indiana hot and humid that makes your shirt damp just walking to the water cooler. I can't remember myself pitching in high school without feeling like I'm drenched in sweat. Not pleasant, I guess, but that's how I remember it. And Dad in front of me and Kristen behind me and no balls and no strikes and no one on.

* * *

There is another cheer and this one is merited because Russell has gotten hold of one and sent it to the base of the wall in right-center. He's hit it almost too hard because it caroms back to the outfielder and Russell has to stop at second instead of going to third. I know it is the World Series and we need the run. And I know the crowd loves him because he smiles and says the right things and he's very, very good. But the best I can manage is indifference. Let Manny hit his home run. I'll take that sliver of hope.

But all the same, I find myself finally paying attention. Russell dances around at second, which is all for show. He isn't going anywhere with two outs and everyone knows it. A hit will score him anyway. Gonzalez is the next batter. He plays first base for us, and we all tease him and call him shortstop. His first name is Alex, which makes him the third Alex Gonzalez to play in the majors. The other two were shortstops. Thus, the joke. Alex is all first baseman, though. We have all of these bruisers in the first half of the lineup. It's ridiculous. Russell is the only one who really looks like an athlete. He exudes ballplayer, but the other three guys just look like piles of rock.

Alex is a good hitter, but he's not as consistent as Russell. He'll chase the high fastball sometimes, but when he hits it, it goes so far that it makes up for it. He's patient and watches the first one go by low for a ball. He lays off the next pitch, too, but it nips the zone. There's another ball and it's two and one and I can tell he wants to swing because he tugs at his pants like he does when he thinks he knows what's coming. Other teams are going to pick up on that soon and he's going to have to stop it. Maybe they already have, or maybe this team has because Guillen throws a high fastball, and it's a foot out of the zone, but Alex swings anyway and he makes contact, but he gets underneath it and pops it way up into the air. Russell starts running like you do when there are two outs and there's nothing else you can do. He crosses home and stands there to watch as Ramirez finds his spot just on the outfield grass behind short and sticks his glove up. The ball claps down into the mitt and that's it for the first inning.

I pop the snaps open on my jacket, slip it off, and grab my glove. Manny finds me on the way out and says, "Don't worry. Just one inning. I tell you, we will score."

"Right, Manny. I know. A home run."

"You got it."

You know, Manny isn't even really that close to me. I mean, he's a nice guy, but we don't have anything in common. He's kind of the talker on the club. And he knows I need it, I guess, so he talks to me and tries to make me smile. Right now it's working. Maybe he can hit a home run.

Brian tosses the ball out to me and I get loose again, but without all the fretting this time. I feel relaxed and I think that maybe tonight it can be like it was. I pretend my sister is standing back there where I know Adam really is. It's just a memory, but it's a good memory. With Kristen behind me and dad in the stands.

Top of the Second.

My illusion vanishes when Jiro Takeda steps to the plate. Unless I missed something, he's the only first baseman Japan has sent to the major leagues, and he is as far from my youth as can be. My high school in rural Indiana had eight hundred kids and seven hundred ninety-six of them were white. That was pretty much true for the schools around us, too. Sometimes, we'd play a team from Indianapolis that was a little more diverse, but it was a lilywhite world for the most part. Dad never liked that, but he didn't care about cultural diversity. He just wanted better competition for me.

Facing Takeda, I have to remember my problem. Dad is not in the stands. But this problem must be secondary. I think Dad would applaud that, even if it means ignoring him. There was a time when his whole life was trying to get me to worry only about the game.

Takeda is good enough to hit third for a lot of teams, but he hits sixth for our opponents. His primary threat is power. He swings freely, but when he makes contact, it's hard. But I am in a groove now and we quickly have him down one ball and two strikes. Brian calls for a fastball and I reach back and let it go. Ninety-eight. I can do that when I want. Takeda can't touch it. Strikeout.

The crowd likes this. I look dominant. I feel dominant. Almost like that second year of college when I was truly untouchable. I can feel the reporters up in the press box writing their ledes. It was a rocky start for Hiatt, and for a moment an entire stadium stood silently on the brink with him before he stepped back to deliver a masterful game and conquer his demons. Perhaps my imaginary article shouldn't be so cocky. There are still some demons to conquer.

The next batter is the left fielder. He's the weak link on the team. No defense to speak of. Just enough offense to not get benched. With three weak hitters in a row, we stick to fastballs and change-ups. Here, we need a single fastball. It is grounded routinely to Adam who shovels it over to first for the second out.

I feel bad when we play National League teams. They have no designated hitter to speak of. At least most of them don't. Usually, we end up facing their fourth outfielder. And let's face it, outfielders don't sit because of their gloves. Tonight is no different as Alex Togneri-Jones steps in against me. We've watched video and talked briefly over him, but I won't lie, he's not someone we've spent much time on. He's left-handed, which is in my favor. He's prone to strike out, which is also in my favor. There is a modest power threat, but it's more of a doubles threat. I settle in and start him with three fastballs that get us to another 1-2 count. Brian calls for a change-up to try and put him away. It almost works. He sends a little bouncer off the end of the bat, Manny has to dive for it and he knocks it down, but the throw doesn't get there in time and suddenly there's a base runner.

This is the kind of thing that used to make me lose it. I did everything right. I should have beaten him and we should be in the dugout now, but instead, I have to pitch to the number nine batter. I'm not scared. I just wanted him leading off the third. Even my first couple of years in majors, I'd melt down about it sometimes and walk the next few batters or give up a homer where I shouldn't. Later, I'd walk into my condo or hotel room and Dad would call—he always called the moment I walked in, and he always said the same thing.

"Hey, I wanted to talk about tonight's game, but I wanted to wait until you were home."

I asked him often enough if he had a GPS implanted in my head or something, but he'd ignore me and launch into a discussion about how it's just baseball and things like that happen and there's no sense getting worked up about things you can't control.

"Now those two guys you walked, you can control that."

Dad was always good at smart little lines like that.

Brian fixed it. I don't know why what he said worked, but Brian is very smart and he knows what to say to all of us. He never messes around with me and I like that. He came in as a free agent during my third year. It was a big signing and people were pretty excited about it. He had a great reputation and he could hit. Anyway, it was the third game of the year—I wasn't quite the number one yet—and a ball got dropped in the outfield. I was marching around behind the mound and Brian called time and trotted out to the mound.

"Zack, do you want to know why you're starting the third game instead of the first?"

"No."

"Because you throw a fit when somebody drops a ball."

"I'm not throwing a fit. It's just frustrating."

"What are you, seven? Be a big boy and get the next out."

He pissed me off a little bit, but I liked that he just said it instead of trying to hold my hand. Anyway, I got the out. Why does everyone think athletes are so fragile? Do they understand what it takes to be a professional athlete? Not everyone has a dad like I did, but I don't know anyone who gets coddled. Sometimes we're full of ourselves, but we all grew up with something, whether it was using a milk carton for a glove or taking grounders in the snow. Most of us don't break easily.

So there's a man on first who shouldn't be, and I'm feeling okay, but I guess Brian is a little nervous. He doesn't normally come out at times like this anymore, but today is different for a couple of reasons, and so he comes out.

"You remember how you used to go all crazy over this stuff?"

"Yeah."

"You're not thinking about doing that now, are you? Cause you look pretty good right now."

"I feel pretty good, too."

"All right then. Let's get out of this inning."

The ninth batter is their second baseman. Jerry Newhall. He looks like he could still be in high school. He's maybe five-eight, and he's on the team for his defense. I throw a fastball inside. He breaks his bat and lifts the least threatening fly ball you've ever seen straight out into center. Three outs. Dad would be proud of me.

Bottom of the Second.

When you play for a very good team, it is easy to forget how good it is. You assume that like most teams, you have a few decent players. Maybe some good hitters in the middle of the order. Maybe one guy in the bullpen who can light up the radar gun. A starter like me. And then a bunch of guys who do their best but aren't great. Will never be considered for an All-Star Game or anything like that. But it isn't true. Our team is ridiculously good and so I should not be surprised that, even though our first four batters hit in the first inning, the rest of our lineup does not go quietly in the second.

It starts with Hector Rivas. I might know less about Hector than anyone on our team. He speaks very little English and he's only twenty-three. He plays left for us, and I guess the thought is that he'll have to move to first eventually because he already doesn't have much range. His bat sure is coming along. He's not the all-around player that Russell is, but he's scarier in some ways. The balls he hits have an extra sharpness to them. Like they could shoot through you if you got in the way. He hits the longest home runs on the team. We played the Reds in interleague this year and he hit one clean into the river. He hit fifth this year only because he's still green. He didn't come up until May of last year. He'll hit third soon. Either because Russell will leave or because he will eventually lose a little something and the second Russell loses something, Hector will be better.

Russell knows this, of course, and has been extra hard on Hector. Last year, Hector got a bunch of the stupid rookie hazing that goes on. Wearing dresses on the plane and that kind of nonsense. That stuff is right up Russell's alley. Anything to make himself feel bigger. The misogyny is just an added bonus.

That is secondary now. Hector wastes no time and he drives the first pitch to the wall. If the angle had been different, it would have been a home run, but it's too low and straight, so it smacks off the wall and Hector ends up at second.

* * *

When I gave up on the dream of smacking a ball like Hector just did, it was a step toward the majors. Dad knew before I did. I've always been the tall, thin kid, and it's hard to be much of a hitter with a strike zone as big as mine. That's what I tell myself. I remember really thinking about it. I always hit seventh or eighth on travel teams. Even on the local rec team, the best I ever did was sixth. I knew I wasn't as good at hitting as some of the other kids. Coaches were always ready to have me pitch, though. They knew there were times when I couldn't hit the broad side of a barn, but, well, you know. A lot of the time I could.

The point is, when I made the decision, it was a real decision. Lots of kids want to be major leaguers in the sixth grade, but they also want to be astronauts and doctors and zookeepers. Being a child is not about deciding. But, in sixth grade, I decided. I had hit a growth spurt and my fastballs were even harder than they had been and you could hear the parents on the opposing team groan when they realized I was pitching. If I could keep it over the plate at all, there was no hope. And anyway, twelve-year-olds will generally swing at almost anything. I was so much better than everyone else that it felt like something I could really do. I let the cat out of the bag one day when Dad asked me if I wanted to take some batting practice. I knew he thought I should pitch, but he was letting me hit. He didn't care, as long as I worked.

"No. I don't really wanna work on my hitting. I'd rather just pitch."

"Why's that?"

"I'm better at pitching than everyone else. I'm not good at hitting."

When I said this, Dad did not have the reaction I expected. He looked at me very seriously and said, "Who're you better than?"

"Everybody."

"Country boys. They're just country boys. They'll be farmers and factory workers and gas station managers. There isn't a real ballplayer in the lot."

"Some of them are pretty good."

"Pretty good when you're twelve doesn't mean squat."

"I still think I could do it."

"Do what?" There was a glimmer in his eye. I realize now that I was just walking into the trap he'd set for me. Hindsight sucks.

"Get drafted. Go to the majors, maybe?"

He softened just a little and said, "You'll have to work hard."

I felt like I was being taken seriously now and I tried to sound grown up. I held a very straight face. "I'll work."

"Okay. Let's finish the rec season first, and then we'll start on the real work."

* * *

Dave Snyder is next. When the designated hitter started, I think Dave is what they had in mind. The older guy who couldn't quite cut it in the field anymore, but could still swing the bat. I like Dave. Everyone likes Dave. He's the guy everyone thinks will be a manager someday. When we have our little kangaroo courts, he's the one who hands out fines and whatnot. Nobody questions him, not even Russell. And if you can get Russell to back off, you're doing something. Dave's knees are shot. Totally shot. He turns doubles into singles. Sometimes he turns triples into singles. He still hit twenty-eight homers this year.

Dave really has the protective older brother vibe to him, so I might be imagining this, but I feel like he's up there trying to give me the lead. He always swings hard, it's not that. There's a look to him. I think there is. Dave always looks like my dad looked when he knew I was really trying. Dad wanted me to be a major leaguer. But he wanted me to work for it. To know that it would take work.

* * *

The mood around the house changed right away. Baseball had always been the biggest thing in our house. Mom was the only one who wasn't obsessed, and even she was a fan. This was something different though. Now, at least when Dad was around, there was nothing else. I had been pitching a lot already. Dad always took every chance to get me to do what he wanted, but this was something different. He brought out all kinds of pitcher-specific workouts. He started having me work in breaking pitches even if I was maybe too young for that. He got hold of all these videos about mechanics and execution and he made me watch them with him over and over again. Whenever we watched a game, the pitchers were all he talked about. If one of them was a lefty, it was even worse.

And poor Kristen. She spent hours providing me with a dummy batter to throw to. Dad almost never let her swing and she would complain to me after about how her arms ached from holding the bat up for so long. She never said anything about it to Dad. I think she saw it as a test. She wanted to believe that if she always did just what he said, eventually he'd start taking the time with her that he was taking with me. I don't know if her commitment would have been as pure if he had pushed her that hard, but I think it would have. Kristen has the mind of a ballplayer. She always has. If the world were fair, she'd be where I am. But it wasn't going to happen, and so she committed herself to whatever Dad was committed to and that meant me. Sometimes she was as hard on me as he was. I think she started to view me as their project more than his project. Nobody ever asked me whose project I thought I was.

* * *

I know for a fact that, right now, most of the team thinks of me as their project. It's kind of a vibe in the dugout. Maybe it was there all along, but I'm noticing it now. They're happy to see me pulling it together. They want to help. Dave almost helps a lot. He hits one deep to center, but a lot of balls to deep center get caught, and this one does. It is enough to move Hector to third and bring up Brian. No one is more on my side than Brian. I know this for certain.

* * *

A lot of athletes are weird about their moms. Most of our moms didn't play sports, but as we got more and more serious, they all learned. The moms can get fervent. Everyone has heard the mom-as-number-one-fan shtick. My mom was never like that. Not the way most people see it. The truth is that she was a big fan of me and she saw that Dad was fervent enough about the baseball player I was becoming for both of them, so she devoted her energy to other things. Mom never actively discouraged me from doing anything I really wanted to do, but she definitely thought I was too young for the pressure Dad was laying on me. Dad couldn't always see beyond himself and I think having a major leaguer for a son appealed to him more than being one himself. If you aren't rich, there's a lot of sacrifice in raising a kid to be ballplayer. We weren't rich. Dad was ready to make the sacrifice and to be applauded for it. It didn't matter that I was eleven. He was ready, and so I was ready. "We'll make it happen." That was what he always said.

All of this is why sixth grade is the first year I can remember both my parents not being at every game. Dad was there, of course. But Mom took some games off. It wasn't mean or anything. It's hard to explain, but she did it so that it was clear she wasn't mad at me and that she didn't think I should stop playing. It was like she wanted to remind me that there was a world outside of baseball. It's hard to convey something that subtle to a kid, but Mom did it.

* * *

Brian has worked a 2-2 count when he connects to tie the game. It's a bouncer to right field. The crowd screams like they haven't since the start of the game. The announcers are almost certainly talking about momentum and turning things around after a rough start, but I'm not thinking about any of that. I'm thinking about Brian. This has been a tough year for him. He's thirty-three, which is starting to get old for a catcher, and he's been hurt a lot this year. He missed all of July and most of August and he probably shouldn't really be playing now, but we don't have better alternatives, and it's hard to tell a player who's gotten you there that he can't play in the World Series.

It's his knees. Just like with Dave. The cartilage is going. He can't really push off and so his power numbers are way down. There are things they could try, but he told me he plans to rest this winter. There's talk of getting him some time at DH next year because Dave might retire. He needs to be more of a hitter for that to be an option, though. He hit worse for us than everyone except Manny this year. He should probably hit eighth, but even Jerry has a heart. Or, at least, he can't forget how Brian hit last year. He'll forget soon. So will Cameron. So will the fans. They'll start talking about "finding catching help" and a year or two later that will be it. He'll hold on as a backup or he'll be gone.

But right now, that is not an issue. Right now, he is dancing around by first and not thinking about his knees. He is smiling and I am smiling. Brian is my best friend. We may not ever play together after this year.

* * *

I think that first year is really the perfect example of how Kristen had the childhood I wanted. She was a freshman in high school and was rejected from every form of organized baseball. That wouldn't hold. The coach would give in. She started the next year, but it was hard for her. Mom and Dad were both understanding. That was part of Mom's disappearance from my games, I think. Kristen didn't want to go to any, which is something I get now, even though it hurt my feelings then, and so Mom would often take her and her friends other places.

I don't think Dad ever knew it, but Mom is how I got into all the gaming stuff. Mom had taken Kristen and a friend of hers to the nearest mall and while they were off being teenagers, she wandered into a hobby store, saw a box of magic cards, and bought them for me. She showed them to me later that day, and I was intrigued. They didn't grab me yet, since I was too busy celebrating all the strike-outs I'd gotten at the game.

I can imagine the fight if Dad had known she was the first one to show that stuff to me. He would have gone on and on about how she had to understand that I had Potential and Needed to Focus. Distractions were to be Minimized. I'm not being flippant when I say that their marriage might not have survived my eighth grade year if he had known.

He didn't know, though. And he drove me hard all through the travel season. We didn't have games or practice every day, but on the days we didn't, Dad came up with something baseball related. This is the first time I remember being unenthusiastic about baseball. He would haul me out into the yard and we would spend hours working on whatever he had decided was important that day. Sometimes he would make me go through my delivery over and over without a ball while making adjustments to my mechanics. When travel season ended, he kept at it. When it got cold, he kept at it. I was eleven. I don't like to think about it. I really don't. I almost never let myself think about it.

* * *

Carver is at bat now. He's the one guy on the team who's friends with Russell. Carver is young and he's just good enough to hold a job. I think he knows he's just stopping in. His destiny is on the bench. Maybe a front office guy later if he plays his cards right. I don't think he's a terrible person, but his association with Russell taints him. He tries too hard to be on everyone's good side. He wants to make sure he has the right friends, but some of us will never trust him because of it. Anyway. He's not much of a hitter because he never makes the pitcher work. His at-bat lasts one pitch. He pops up and Brian stands on the bag and watches it drop into the glove of the second baseman. The crowd gets quiet because they know Manny is coming up, and fun as he is, you don't count on Manny for theatrics in the batter's box. They are resigning themselves to a tie game when a few moments ago, they were thinking about grabbing the lead. I understand.

* * *

Hard as I try to keep it down, there's one memory that keeps coming back from that first year of hard training. It was January and it was cold. There was snow and outside looked desolate. Where I grew up in Indiana, it's very flat. Not far to the south of us, hills rise up, but where I was, it's just open. This is especially true in the winter, when the fields all lie empty. You can see for miles and there's nothing. It was especially cold out and I just wasn't feeling it when Dad dragged me outside for practice.

"I don't want to work out today, Dad. It's too cold."

"Oh, it's too cold, huh? What if the Rockies draft you and it's snowing on Opening Day and they want you to pitch?"

He paused, but I didn't say anything, so he went on.

"You going to turn down an Opening Day start because it's cold? Real good. Kiss the free agent money goodbye. Nobody wants a pitcher who won't pitch. And you're not even there yet. You're just a kid, and you're already packing it in. I thought you wanted to be a major leaguer."

"I do." I knew I was losing.

"Then you gotta work, kid."

"But it's so cold. How cold does it have to be to not come outside and practice?"

Dad smiled like he knew this was coming. Like he'd been waiting for it. He pointed over the house where the kitchen window was. Outside it, there were some bird feeders that my mom kept because she liked to watch them in the winter. She said it reminded her of spring. "You see your mom's birds there?"

"Yeah."

"You know what they are?"

"I know the cardinals."

"There are some cardinals there. Chickadee. Nuthatches. Goldfinch, too. And a bunch of sparrows in a group there. They're all pretty if you look at them long enough, even when they don't have their colors. They're here all year."

"So."

"So, if you look outside and there's no cardinal. No chickadee. No pretty little goldfinch. If you can't hear a sparrow singing, then you can stay inside."

He paused for effect.

"But if I can see a goldfinch or I can hear a sparrow, you better be ready to work or stop wasting my time."

* * *

Manny is serious about trying to hit a home run. I hadn't been thinking about it, but he has the crowd going. He keeps fouling off balls and he's swinging hard. This is not his game, but it's getting loud. The fans like it. I'd like it if I was a fan, but I know he should be trying to poke a single through the infield. That's our best hope. But he wants the lead. He wants to give me—to give all of us—a charge. I get caught up in it, too. He's sending lasers into the stands over and over. He's behind everything because he's trying to kill it, but he keeps getting the bat on the ball. That's the one thing Manny has going for him. He struck out only fifty times this year, and that's a bad year for him. He gets the bat on the ball, even if it doesn't go very far. He keeps at it long enough that he is doing us a service by pumping up Guillen's pitch count. I'm not counting, but I know he's seen ten or twelve pitches before he finally gets one in play, and I'll give him credit, he gets it out there farther than he usually does. Down a line and it might have a chance, but it just dies out in right-center and that's the end of the inning.

* * *

There are times in Indiana when you really can't play. We get thunderstorms. And in the winter it can get really nasty sometimes. Lots of snow and then nasty wind across the fields. The sparrows don't come out in that.

I hated Dad sometimes for pushing me so hard. I was too young then. In high school I maybe could have taken it, but not then. It took a long time to fix things between us, but there were times every winter, no matter how hard Dad was pushing me, when we'd find ourselves snowed in for a week with nothing to do and we'd look outside and stare at the snow for a minute and one of us would say, "I wish it were baseball season." Then we'd go off to the living room and watch one of the old games Dad had recorded or maybe the Baseball documentary. That was always there. Even when I was in eighth grade and tried to make Dad hate me, we still watched the entire documentary together that winter. I haven't thought about some of this stuff in years. It doesn't make sense—the stuff from when I was a kid. I can see only two pictures. I can see the overbearing father who made me feel awful and I can see Dad sitting next to me on the couch talking about Ted Williams or Hank Aaron. And I'm sitting there listening and I'm enchanted. Or we are at a game together and by this time, I'm into it when Dad is talking and coaching me because I see the game more fully than when I was little and I love it. Or I'm in a field wishing the birds would leave the feeder because it's cold and there are a couple of inches of snow on the ground and I'd rather do just about anything than practice baseball, but he won't let me go in. He never touches me. Never physically forces me, but the way he talks to me isn't much different. He takes the choice away from me and I hate him and I hate baseball. I am twenty-eight years old and I don't understand how both of these versions can be true. Those two men seem too far apart to be the same, and yet I know they are.

Top of the Third.

I've gone through the lineup once and intro-
ductions have been made. I have a tie score and a
clean slate. Ramirez twitches his shoulders, pulls
at his batting gloves and steps in. For the second
time tonight, he begins his piston-bounce. I am
intimidated. If anyone has a mental advantage
on me tonight, it's Ramirez. I don't want him on
base again. He's too disruptive. I am determined
to start with a strike, but just like the first time, I
miss with a fastball.

Brian throws the ball back to me and I march
around behind the mound. I blow out a breath,
watch it condense in the air, and climb back up the
hill. Brian is calling for a slider. This, I know, is

how he shows confidence in me. "You missed with the first one? So what. Let's show him what you've got." I nod and try to relax. I wind up and the pitch sails in and Ramirez lashes it foul down the right field line. He spits and steps back into the box and starts his bounce. He stares out at me. He's not scared. He should be scared. I can throw hard. But he's not scared. We try fastball again. Again he watches it go past for a ball. Brian calls change-up, hoping to fool Ramirez, but it doesn't work. He sends a hard one-hopper to third. From where I stand, I know before anyone else that he'll be on base. There's a hard bounce in the infield dirt and a cloud of dust flies up. Carver punches his glove over and snags the ball, but it's moving so fast, it knocks him to the ground. He pops up quickly and zips it across the diamond. Even with the good throw, it's not much of a contest. Ramirez is well past the bag by the time the ball thwacks into Alex's glove. He is on base. Again.

I am nervous. He is the leading run and he is on base. Coates is up next. I don't feel nervous about him. The first time wasn't about him, it was about me. But Ramirez. Ramirez is different. I throw over to first and he gets back standing. He looks at me and I think I see a smirk. "Try harder." His uniform is still clean, but I know it won't stay that way. I do try harder when I throw over a second time and he has to dive back. It's close, and I almost get him, but it feels like a mistake. It feels like I have given him what he wants. Gotten his blood flowing. I throw over a third time and he dives back again, but he dives because he wants to, not because he has to. Finally, I start toward the plate for the first pitch to Coates. Ramirez is off the moment I twitch. I know he's been watching tape of me, trying to parse my movements, but his jump is so good I wonder if he's found a tell. Brian makes a hell of a throw, but it doesn't matter. Ramirez is popping up from the bag by the time the ball gets there.

I stare back at the bag with my hands on my hips. He looks at me and bounces around on second. He is in my head and he knows it. The crowd has been with me, but a crowd can be fickle and now they are quiet. Ramirez isn't going to make the first out trying to steal third, so I focus on the batter. This time, I expose him for who he is. Two more fastballs and a change-up are all it takes and he is gone on strikes.

Mike Ferris steps to the plate and I am reminded of Brian a few years ago. Catchers rarely move quickly, but there's a deliberateness to the stride of the younger ones. Sometime in their thirties, they all lose it. The movement of the lower body goes from deliberate to tentative. Gingerly. Brian moves like that now, but Ferris is still a train or a bear or whatever your preferred metaphor is for something large and scary. I catch myself admiring him and force myself to stop. There isn't time for this kind of wistfulness. I need to focus on Ferris because he can hurt me. He gets talked about like

Bench or Piazza and that is not hyperbole. He will crush the ball if I make a mistake. And there is still Ramirez dancing around back there. With a hitter like Ferris up, you'd expect him to sit still and wait to be driven in. Most runners would sit still, but Ramirez is different. Maybe he is going, maybe he isn't. Still, he dances. He wants to mess with me. He wants me to be scared. I am scared. To be scared of someone so small feels absurd. I tell myself not to worry, but I'm not good at telling myself anything today. This is the kind of day when I should already be expecting a call from Dad, no matter how the rest of the game goes. "What was going on with Ramirez? So he got on base? So what. Pitch to Ferris. Ferris can hurt you more than Ramirez." Today, I might tell Dad he was wrong. A thousand small cuts can do the job as well as a bomb. The only difference is the mess.

I need to be deadly with Ferris. If he gets a hit, Ramirez will score. If he doesn't, then the odds get better fast. Maybe Ramirez ends up at third, but with two outs, I can probably get out of it.

I try to be perfect. Brian calls for a fastball and sets up over the inside corner. I miss and it is a ball. Brian calls for a slider and I miss again and we are down and I have to get a strike. Fastball again, middle-in. Ferris fouls it off. Two and one is a little better, but I'm not out of the woods. It's time to change paces on him, so Brian calls for a change-up. My change-up is good. Sometimes, it gets down into the seventies. We're hoping to get him out in front and even up the count. But Ferris is smart. He's guessed along with us and is not fooled. What happens next is not believable.

Ferris swings and he hits the ball hard, but he's just a little over the top. It zips along the ground. Against most teams, it would be a single into left, but we have Manny. Manny dives and stops it. He is back up so fast it's like he was never down. He plants and throws and if Ferris is a bear, then this throw is a bullet strong enough to down an elephant. It isn't close. Ferris is out by half a dozen steps. Ramirez, I know, won't have been slowed down by the left-side grounder. I turn around expecting to see him at third, but he is already half way home. Players take risks like this sometimes and Ramirez saw how I put them away in the second. He knows they might not get another shot and he is taking the chance. This time, I am doomed to be behind on the play. Alex has seen him before I have, and when I turn back, the ball is already coming out of his hand. The throw is a little bit to the wrong side of the plate and it slows the tag just enough. Brian dives across to try and tag Ramirez, but it's no good. He's safe and we are losing again.

Brian thinks he got the out and he pops up to argue. Jerry pops out of the dugout to argue. It's the third inning. Why are they making a stink like this? Is it me? Are they worried about me? He was safe. I saw him slide in. I saw the tag land late. Safe. I can see the umpire starting to bristle. Brian and Jerry are both really going. Profanity is starting to fly. That's not going to be good. It's the World Series, and they're losing their heads. If Brian got tossed it would be a disaster. I go to him and start pulling him away.

"I tagged him!"

"You were late."

"The hell I was."

"Hey, idiot, you were late. I saw. Back off before you get tossed!" This snaps him out of it. Jerry has also calmed down and starts back toward the dugout, kicking at the baseline as he crosses it.

All of this—Ramirez, Jerry, Brian—has made me angry. I am the one who is supposed to lose his head tonight. I am the one who needs to be kept cool. I am the one who is supposed to take stupid risks. This is an unreasonable world and an unreasonable game. The crowd is fired up now because they think Jerry and Brian showed guts or spark or something. Screw them, too. They don't know. They don't know how stupid it is to lose your head. How it never leads to anything except a few good quotes for the press later on. And if anyone loses it, it should be me. Here comes Martin. Let's get it.

Brian puts down a one and I nod and reach back and I let it go. I'm not aiming at Martin, but it looks like I am. He goes down and the ball thumps against the backstop. The whole place goes silent. The umpire steps out from behind the plate and takes a few steps out like they do sometimes when they want to seem important and he points at me and he points at the benches. This is our warning. He thinks I did it on purpose. Martin is glaring at me like he wants to eat me. I can see his hands gripping the bat like he would maybe like to grip my neck. Now I want to hit him, but I know I can't. I know that much.

Brian asks for the fastball again and sets up outside. I reach back and I throw as hard as I can. I've scared Martin and he takes a little defensive swing and pops it up into shallow center where just about anyone can get to it and where Manny finally does glove it. Martin stares at me as he walks back to the dugout, but I won. He knows I won and that is the end of things. That was routine. Normal. As we jog back to the dugout, I call Brian something I wouldn't repeat in front of my mother. He doesn't say anything, but he gives me a look. A sad look. And I know what it means. I know that all of that was for me. And do you know how that makes me feel? It makes me feel like shit. I wish I could take it all back. I wish we weren't losing again.

Bottom of the Third.

I put on my jacket, go down to the end of the bench, sit by myself, and continue to feel bad.

Adam is walking up to the plate. Tasked, once again, with leading the attempt to pull us even after I have given up a run. It's only the third inning, there is still a long way to go, and it is only two to one, but it feels insurmountable. It feels like we might battle back. Pull even. Find the leading run on second and fool ourselves for a minute. But we will lose. This is what I believe. No matter that I believe we should win, with this team facing me, with our team against this pitcher. We should win this game. We are better than them. We should win. But we will fail.

Adam does not look like he feels this way. He looks like he believes, still. What will happen if we tie again or take the lead? Will I surrender it? When will I surrender it?

* * *

The night it happened, we were on a plane. I heard as soon as we landed. I had a frantic message from Mom. Brian noticed me calling her back, and he stayed back on the plane while everybody else was filing off. I can't think about Mom's voice then. I can't think about what she said. If I do, I won't be able to function. What I remember now, sitting on the bench waiting for the inning to start, is that Brian stayed back with me. That he had the sense to remember that there was a huge crowd outside waiting for us. Waiting for me. The winning pitcher. They wanted to see me and cheer for me. None of them knew. Nobody knew yet except Brian. Soon, it would be all over the news, but right now, it was just a bunch of tired and happy fans, all of them clothed in team colors and championship shirts and hats, many of them a little drunk.

Only a few hours before, I'd been looking forward to it. I'd thrown a fantastic game. Two hits in eight innings. I would have gone out for the ninth, but we were up five, so there was no need. Afterward, we'd celebrated, but not too hard. Most of the team was here last year when we lost in the LCS. This was nice, but it was only a step toward the larger goal. Win it all. Win the Series. So yeah, we put on our hats and t-shirts. We drank some beers, but we weren't jumping all around like fools. That was to be saved for later.

But boarding the plane, there was still a tingle. We knew what kind of crowd would greet us, the conquering heroes. We knew it would be great. It would have been great.

"Oh God. Oh God. I can't go out there Brian. I can't go out there. You have to make them go away." I was in shock and I was starting to shake.

"They are not going away. Not any time soon. You're going to have to walk out there."

"I just want to be alone. I don't want to be with all those people."

He put his hands on my shoulders so that I had to look at him. "Zack, those people are not going away. All you have to do is smile and wave. I'll drive you home myself. I'll stay if you want. But for just a minute, you need to pretend. Be the cliché."

I nodded. I wiped my eyes and blew my nose and tried to stop crying for a minute. I tried to make myself feel how I normally feel starting a game. I looked down at the ground and shook myself out. I bounced like a prizefighter entering the ring. I let Brian lead. We stepped outside and the roar was instant. I jerked my head up and shot a fist up into the air. I danced down the step and onto the tarmac. I smiled and waved. I high-fived as we wandered past. I signed a few autographs. A couple of people saw the strain in my eyes. They looked at me like something was wrong and when they did this, I tried to smile more. We got through the crowd. I got in Brian's car and he started it and drove us both away.

* * *

The crowd is cheering and I look up to see Adam rounding first. He comes into second not with a slide, but with the kittenish stutter-step of a sure arrival. He claps his hands together and I watch him take off his gloves and run them over to the first base coach. The crowd. The crowd. The crowd. They believe. They won't know until later. They will ride it and they will roar and they will believe and we will disappoint them.

* * *

Brian stayed up with me that night. We talked a lot. I told him stuff nobody else knows. I don't have a wife or girlfriend to tell that stuff to. A lot of it is pretty terrible. After we'd been talking for most of the night, Brian asked why I even still talked to my dad.

"I don't know. I didn't for a while. When I went to college, I was out of his jurisdiction. I was on scholarship. There was nothing he could do to me. He'd always call. He'd drive up for my games when he could. But I ignored him. Brushed him off the phone. Didn't talk to him after games."

"What changed?"

"It's funny because I only went to college at his insistence. I got drafted out of high school, but it was sixth round. Not a ton of bonus money or anything. Scouts didn't like the competition I faced and they'd gotten the impression I was soft. Dad had a hand in that. Dad said if I went to college, I could show them. He said I'd go first round."

"He was right about that."

"That was when I called Dad. I mean, I had an agent. I didn't need Dad to negotiate, but he made me a lot of money pushing me to go to college, and I felt bad because I'd never told Dad he was right before. And I kind of missed him, too. It wasn't always so bad. When I was a kid, you know?"

"You remember the first time your dad takes you to a game?"

I smiled at him and let him talk.

"And there's all this food and it smells so good."

I laughed. "I didn't understand why we weren't allowed out on the field."

Brian laughed.

"My first game wasn't even a big league game. We didn't have the money for those a lot, but we could always drive to Indy or Louisville for a minor league game. The first one I can remember was in Louisville, I think. It was in this terrible stadium the football team down there used. Astro-turf. Fairground stands. You know what I'm talking about?"

Brian nodded.

"We were way up, even though the place was mostly empty. I wanted to move closer, but Dad had us in those seats on purpose. He wanted me to see the whole field. But we were so far away the players were like ants. I was probably only five or six. I just got bored."

I guess I looked kind of depressed about it or something because Brian asked me if I still felt bad about it.

"No. It's a good memory. Dad was really patient. I mean, I didn't even know how to read the score-board yet."

"What do you mean?"

"The stadium only had a board that showed runs, hits and errors. And I just read the three together as one big number. Like I thought it was four eighty-two to two forty. I remember a guy hit a homer and I asked Dad how come they got two hundred points and he just laughed and explained it to me."

* * *

With Adam standing at second, I stare down the bench at Brian. He is looking at me. When he sees me glance in his direction, he gets up and walks toward me.

"I'm sorry, man."

"It's fine."

"I'm pretty messed up right now."

"I know."

"Anyway, what are you doing trying to get thrown out of the game?" I try to say this so he will laugh. He smiles at least.

"Fine. I won't try to get outs for you anymore."

"Yeah, because arguing safe calls with an umpire has ever worked."

"First time for everything."

It's not much, but it's enough. With Brian sitting next to me, I'm able to see the romance of the game a little better. It's still cold out, but Brian always sweats in his catcher gear and his hair is wet from it. He wears eye black for reasons that completely escape me as he hasn't had to worry about the outfield sun since Little League. His shin guards are scuffed. I look at Brian and I look at Adam standing out at second base and I think maybe I am wrong and we are not doomed to defeat. It would be a good story. I wouldn't mind reading it, probably, in twenty or thirty years. The time Dad died, but I won a World Series game anyway. If I hadn't pitched, Brian wouldn't be here next to me. No one would be talking to me. I wouldn't really be part of the team, even if I did have a uniform on.

Matt comes up and for the first time tonight, I feel impelled to watch the game. I stand and move to the railing. I have that tense hyper-aware feeling I get sometimes when I'm excited about a game. My hand rubs against the cross bar and I feel all the places where the paint has chipped off and been repainted and chipped again. I put myself in Matt's head, which is a nice place to be.

One of the best things about Matt is how levelheaded he is. It may be the World Series and we may really need this run, but he knows Guillen isn't the greatest pitcher in the world and he knows better than to panic and hack at everything in hopes of driving in the run. He works the count beautifully. And gets to three and two. Guillen is better off missing outside the zone than in. Matt knows this and he sits still and watches ball four go past him. He is about to toss his bat and trot to first when the umpire calls strike three.

I can tell it gets to him. It's a bad enough call that it'd get to me if I were hitting and pitchers do not ever complain about a bigger strike zone. But it's not worth arguing. Matt says exactly what he always says when he doesn't like a call, "I disagree." It's hilarious. He always plays it straight. He never yells, and then he walks back to the dugout. It works, though. Matt gets a lot more strikes called as balls than balls called as strikes.

Still, it hurts to have the first out and Adam stationary at second. But here comes everyone's favorite hero. Russell. There's always hope when he's at bat. For my part, I lose interest in the game and go back to sit with Brian.

"You think pretty boy there will bail you out tonight?"

"I don't know if I want him to." When I say this, Brian gives me a disapproving look. He probably feels the same way, but you're not supposed to say it.

* * *

If anything makes me sick about the industry that is major league baseball, it is the success of Russell Jennings. Russell, unlike most major leaguers, has national endorsements. Russell is beloved nationally as a stand-up guy for the work he does—or pretends to do—for charity. Russell is a Hall of Fame player if he stays healthy. Russell is beloved by the media and the fans. Most of us hate him.

That hatred is fairly new. Russell was never especially likable. When the cameras are off, he's full of himself and standoffish. We could put up with that, of course, as long as he played. And he definitely plays. Gold Glove last year. Batting title. Thirty-five homers a year. Yes, you can be a jerk if you put up those numbers. I don't even care if you play the media game and turn on the smiles and charming quotes for the cameras.

But what happened this spring was something else.

* * *

If Russell has a flaw as a player it is that he craves glory. In this situation, he knows what a home run will do. It will guarantee him a mention in the recaps and wrap-ups, even if we lose. If we win, it makes him the star of the game unless I strike out the next eight or nine batters. Guillen's first pitch is a strike, but it's not Russell's pitch. He should know better and lay off, but he takes a big hack and misses. Lucky for him. If he'd put it in play, he'd be out on a routine grounder.

After that aggressive swing, Guillen and Ferris are looking to get him to chase. Guillen goes to his curve, which is really good when he's on, and lets the bottom drop out so that it bounces and Ferris has to block it. There is no concern about the ball getting by Ferris and sending Adam to third. Balls do not get by Ferris. Russell isn't biting. He's aggressive, but he's not stupid. One ball and one strike.

* * *

There are plenty of ballplayers who are not what you'd call respectful of women. I don't think it's most of us, but it's not an insignificant piece of the major league population. These are the guys who have a different girl in every city. Sometimes more than one girl. It goes on. It's not nice. You sure don't want them hitting on your sister. But it's part of the deal. You look the other way. And really, what can you do? Trash talk them to the media? That would not make for a happy team. And, "Twenty-something guy with money sleeps around" isn't a surprising headline.

We thought Russell was one of these guys for a while. By which I mean, we thought he had women everywhere. We'd all seen him turn on the charm with some girl in the stands before a game just like he did with the media. He'd finish his batting practice with a long homer and then saunter over. He'd casually sign autographs for a few kids to set the stage, then a few minutes later, he'd walk away with her phone number. He'd text her from the dugout. If there were no reporters around, he'd do this while saying exactly the kinds of things you'd expect to whomever would listen. Usually Carver. It was gross. But nothing to be done.

Then this girl, Anne White, accused him of raping her. My reaction, and the reaction of most everyone on the team, was "Well, of course he did." It wasn't hard to believe. He was a jerk. He used women. He liked to be in charge. It was obvious.

But the fans weren't having it. Signs at the ballpark supporting him. Footage on the news of people saying she must be lying to try and get money out of him. Baseball writers focused on whether the "allegations" would affect his on-field performance. Pretty much nobody thought about the girl. Craig Calcaterra is the only one I can remember who said something along the lines of, "Hey, a woman might have been raped here. And you know, people don't lie about this stuff often."

I get that it hurts when your favorite player turns out to be an actual bad person, but being a human should matter too.

* * *

On the third pitch, Russell almost gets the RBI he wants. Almost. He hits a hard line drive, but there is Ramirez diving to catch it. Adam just barely gets back to second in time. I feel Brian twitch next to me. He fidgets in his seat. "Damn," he says, because he wants to win more than he hates Russell. And I know I shouldn't be happy. We are trying to win the World Series, and I am definitely trying to win the game. But the hate is a little more for me than it is for Brian. It's almost enough to not care about winning. Almost.

* * *

But I'm pretending I couldn't have been one of the apologists. High school locker room talk is not that different from major league locker room talk. There's a sense that what's said there isn't public. You watch it a little more as a pro, but still, your guard is down.

Kristen tried out for the high school team during her freshman year and got cut, but sophomore year, she was too good and they had to keep her. She had a really hard time. She managed to straddle the line between conventionally attractive and athletic and the boys on the team didn't know how to behave. She was supposed to start at second, but she came home crying from practice one day. She wouldn't talk to me or Dad, but she told Mom what happened. I learned much later that there had been some grabbing. That she'd been held up against a wall where the coaches couldn't see.

Mom told Dad, and then Dad came out of their room with his mouth set hard. He didn't look at me at all, which was strange because I was used to being the center of his world. He bent down and gave Kristen a hug. "I have to go out for a little bit," he said. "But I won't be gone long."

Again, oblivious as I was, I didn't figure out until way later that he went to the coach's house. When he came home, I don't think it was even an hour later, he told Kristen that she shouldn't have any more trouble and to let him know if she did.

I was in my first year of college when something came up with another player on the team. I was talking to Kristen about how he was a good guy and I didn't see how he could have done it.

"Oh, they're always nice guys. Or they pretend to be."

"No, he really is. He said she changed her mind afterward."

"Okay."

"What?"

"Don't you know what happened to me in high school?"

"What are you talking about?"

She told me. And other stuff too. I guess it had mostly blown over by the time I got to school, but for a couple of years, she was left alone by the team when she was around, but they still talked. I guess they said she was a tease. It gave her a reputation at school and she got harassed for it.

"Which was stupid for every reason you can think of," she said.

"What does that have to do with this, though?"

"Come on, Zack. Don't be so thick. What could this woman possibly gain from lying about it?"

"I don't know."

"Exactly."

And then she hung up on me. Later that night I got a long email with a bunch of links and, well,

I suddenly found it awfully hard to believe my teammate, even if he was nice.

* * *

Gonzalez is up now, but the air has gone out of the stadium. With two outs, it's a hit or nothing if we want to score. A pretty good hit, too. Adam's not a snail, but he's not scoring on a standard issue single.

* * *

The guy at school eventually got off with just a reprimand, which is pretty much normal. Shameful as that is. That guy, at least, had the sense to deny it to everyone. Russell can't be bothered to go that far. When somebody asked him about it all he said was, "What did she think was going to happen? A ballplayer's hotel room on the road? How's she gonna change her mind then? She wouldn't have been there if she didn't want it." The sad thing is, it just shows he was smart enough to know that's what everyone else would think.

* * *

I'll give Alex credit; he's going at it just as hard as everyone else. Guillen is lucky to still have the lead, and I suspect he knows it. If things break just a little differently, there are two men on, no outs, a run in, and a couple of scary hitters coming up. Baseball is funny like that. Lots of guys, especially TV guys, will tell you that there is no luck in baseball, but I don't know how they explain an inning like this. A ball four called a strike. A liner that can be caught only by Ramirez or Manny. I mean, yeah, there's some skill there, but it's easy to see Guillen on the ropes. It's easy to imagine us putting up three, four, five runs. Maybe even putting the game out of reach.

Dad was smart enough to know that. It was actually kind of funny to be around him when an announcer started going on about controlling the direction of the ball off the bat.

"Ninety-five mile per hour fastball, and this idiot wants it two feet further to the right. Unbelievable."

Alex is up there giving it his all. I've lost track of how many pitches he's seen, but it's been a full count for a while. Maybe we don't score this inning, but we'll see the bullpen an inning earlier than we would have otherwise. I always laugh at the old-school managers who want their players swinging. What was it Baker said once? Clogging the bases. Yeah. Don't clog the bases against me. Swing those bats. Our guys don't do that. Patient as can be. Watching Alex, or any of our first seven really, makes me glad I pitch for this team so I don't have to face them.

I am thinking this when I hear Russell grumbling down at the other end of the dugout.

"Any other team, and this game is tied."

"Not against me," Manny says.

"Shut up, Manny."

Every silver lining has a cloud.

* * *

Dad came down to spring training this year for a few days, just to visit and be around baseball, and we were having a beer one night when I told him what Russell said.

"You tell anyone about that?" he asked.

"No." I couldn't tell what he thought I should have done.

"You think it would do any good?"

"I don't know."

"Well, somebody will probably be around to talk to you all. When they come, tell the truth. It might not matter, but at least you'll have done what you can."

He was right. A few days later, the DA sent someone down for due diligence. I told him what Russell said, and I'll never forget his response, "Well, Jennings has a point there." That's when I knew it was hopeless.

I called Dad that night. He wasn't surprised. I asked him if he remembered the thing with Kristen in high school.

"Sure I remember."

"What'd you do when you left the house?"

"I asked the coach what he thought about it. He said that was why he'd cut her during her freshman year. Said she had to expect that kind of thing."

"What an asshole."

"Yup."

"So what changed?"

"I asked him if he knew about my son."

"Of course he knew about me. What does that have to do with anything?"

"Well, he was counting on having you pitch in a couple of years. I never told you this, but he wanted to move you up early. I wasn't having it. I wanted you to progress naturally. I told him I wasn't going to have my son learning those kinds of values and if the coach couldn't keep his own players in line, he'd be out a second baseman and the best pitching prospect south of Indy."

"Wow."

"Meant it, too. I'd have found somewhere for you to play. You were too good for that little school anyway."

The way he said it made it clear that he never had any doubts about how things would go. Dad was always good at having his cake and eating it, too. He would have held me out if the coach hadn't budged. He would have found the money for a serious travel team. But he knew he wouldn't have to. Together, Kristen and I made the team a regional contender and one not to be taken lightly at state. Without us, they were nothing special. Coaches in small towns have to grab opportunity when it comes or they might not see it again.

* * *

But our opportunities are done, at least for now. Alex badly mishandles a curveball and grounds out to third. The stadium has a dissatisfied hum like a too-full restaurant with bad service. Brian stands up off the bench like an old man and grunts as he climbs the steps. I wait a moment for the others to take the field and wonder if the moment of hope I felt was an illusion.

Top of the Fourth.

Not every moment in a baseball game is filled with urgency, even if that game is part of the World Series. A lot of fans would flip out if I said this in public. They would insist that it is never appropriate to relax (unless they were telling me I was too tense). Every play must be filled with intensity. They would double down on this in the playoffs and mortgage their house on it in the World Series. They would talk about mental toughness, and the especially unaware might even mention grit. These people are idiots.

For three innings, this game has been a roller coaster. We lost the first game, and we are losing by a run in this one. I should be concerned. I should know that it is imperative that I pitch at my best. Whatever. I'm tired. Already, I am tired. I just want to pitch. I want to stare in at Brian, throw what he calls for and watch the game unfold. I don't care if I miss the mark a little. I just want to play and get through the inning and go back to the dugout. I want to shut my eyes and let my head fall back with a low thud against the concrete wall in the dugout.

Though you might not believe it, all of these feelings are good. I get myself to this place often enough during the regular season. I suppose I'm not that different from Nook LaLoosh. Except, perhaps, that I look like I know how to throw. I do my best work when I am unconcerned. Baseball is a game of ritual and it is best performed through ritual. Tonight, I have been slow to arrive, but as I take the mound, I want nothing more than to escape into ritual.

But the ball is so damn cold.

Little things can destroy ritual, and it's awfully hard to get a physical grip on the ball. Like all pitchers, I'm most comfortable when the hide of the ball gives under my fingers and I am hot enough for the sweat from my hands to moisten it slightly. Even the way the mound feels when my front foot lands is different in the cold. I have to work to keep the ritual tonight. I grip the ball a moment longer to let it warm. I blow onto my hand. And the best part, the part that keeps me going, is that the act of pitching—the windup, the cocking of the arm, the jolt as I release the ball—is always the same. It does not matter if it is cold or hot or raining. It is motion. Only motion. It is motion I have repeated thousands upon thousands of times. It is ritual.

I am enmeshed in the ritual as Mauricio Apolinar steps to the plate for his second at-bat. I was not intimidated by him in the second inning, and I am not intimidated by him now. Though, in fairness, I am not anything right now. I watch Brian closely. I nod. I grip. I pitch. I do not even register the kind of pitches I am throwing. I skip the conscious part of my brain. I am merely action. I throw five pitches to Apolinar before he lifts a low fly ball gently to right. Matt glides up to grab it easily.

The ball is tossed into the infield, around the horn, and back to me. Takeda steps back to the plate. I settle in, nod at Brian, throw what he calls for. The pitch dives away from him before I know it's a nasty slider I've thrown. He waves at it. I continue to follow Brian's directions and after two more pitches, Takeda swings at another slider and strikes out.

The crowd cheers for the strikeout like we've just clinched the Series. I don't know why, but they do. Brian pops up and throws the ball back with a little extra English on it. I find myself smiling and laughing. They continue to cheer. It is such a strange moment. Can they see how calm I've become? Is it so obvious? Are they only desperate?

No, it's not desperation. I can hear that much. They were just happy and somehow it's gotten contagious and they can't stop. I look around and everyone is smiling or chuckling. Alex, Adam, Manny. I look at Manny and ask what's going on. He shrugs that he doesn't know. I do the only thing I can think to do. I tip my cap. They cheer even louder. It's just a strikeout. It's not even the end of the inning, but still they cheer. The ump is gesturing that it's time to get back to it.

I haven't even mentally acknowledged the name of the left fielder yet, but I know it. It's impossible to forget, feeling so out of place in the modern game. Art Lynch. He sounds like someone who should have played in the thirties. The scrappy bench guy for the Yankees. Cheering for Babe Ruth and Lou Gehrig.

Then or now, he's not much to be concerned with. I feel bad, sometimes, about the how dismissive I am of certain hitters, and they do burn me at times. Of course, they do. Even a poor major league hitter is still a major league hitter, but I can't be bothered to worry about players I shouldn't worry about. I only have so much energy.

So yes, Lynch. Here he is. I lean forward, my arm dangles. I nod at the signal, throw the asked-for fastball, and watch a foul ball skitter down the first base line and bounce up into the stands. A new ball is tossed to me. My arm dangles. Another fastball. A strike looking. Another fastball and an awkward swing and miss. Only three pitches this time—sometimes it really is that easy—and that's it. Out of the inning.

And they are cheering again. I trot to the dugout and sit down, but they won't stop. This is ridiculous. We're losing, but it doesn't feel like it. So I pop my head out again and tip my cap again and the fans roar. All day, I have felt empty, but suddenly, I feel so full I might cry. This is a display of love, and they have no reason to love me other than the color of my shirt. Still, it fills me up, this easy love, and I have to sit down and bury my face. My undershirt is damp despite the cold, the sweat has started to gather. A bead runs down the side of my cheek. I think it is sweat. It could be a tear. I don't know. If it were always like this, I'd never leave. I close my eyes and listen.

Bottom of the Fourth.

There is something in the air right now. I don't know what it is. I am not one for superstition or romance, even where the World Series is concerned. I believe in baseball. Usually the best team wins, but anything can happen and usually doesn't mean always.

But still, tonight, all of a sudden, there is something. Hector steps in and even though he is a mystery, I still love him. I love him because he is not Russell and because he is so young he makes me feel old and wise. Guillen winds up, and the first pitch floats in and even I can see where this is going. Hector sees it perfectly, he rears back like he's hitting off a tee and the ball just goes and goes and goes. He hits it to dead center and there's still not a question. Coates doesn't even move. The game is tied.

I thought the crowd was loud before, but that was nothing. It's like they're willing us to win. That's stupid. I know it's stupid. I know we have to do it, but that's what it feels like. Hector gets around the bases like he's afraid he'll be caught. His foot stomps on home plate and I swear I can feel the smack of it down in the dugout. We all stand and cheer and high-five him. The crowd roars and roars. And now Hector has to take a curtain call. Tied. We are tied. For the first time all night, I wish Dad was here just so he could see. I mean, I don't want him here for me. I just want him to see the game. To see how good it is right now. He was never a screamer, but I think he might now. I think he might.

* * *

Somehow, when I entered high school, Dad got himself appointed as an assistant coach. He had no connection with the school other than Kristen and me. Having grown up in the next county over, he hadn't even gone to school there. But, well, as I've said, Dad had a way of getting what he wanted, and in little country high schools where sports matter more than they have any right to, things can be arranged.

Strangely, Dad would never come all the way clean about how he managed it. Unless you believe the explanation he gave, which I don't. All he said was that they saw the talent he had produced and asked him to help out. I think it had something to do with the threat he'd made a few years earlier. Our head coach tolerated Dad, but he never warmed all the way.

I do know he did it for free. He never had a uniform, and I guess he was never officially a coach. He always sat in the stands for games because that was a line our head coach wouldn't let him cross, but he was there every practice and was allowed on the field when no one else was.

It took a long, long time for me to admit it, but I ended up glad that he managed it. It was a good thing for me, even if it wasn't always a good thing for the team.

* * *

And now Dave is up and as he stands there gripping the bat, I swear he is looking dead at me. He waits on the first pitch and it is a ball. He waits on the second pitch and it is a strike. He waits on the third pitch and it is a ball. He looks like he knows what's coming. I remember how lucky Guillen was last inning. I remember suddenly that John has been very active, walking around, talking to the hitters. As I remember this, Dave whacks a ball to the base of the outfield wall. It bounces around enough that even on his bad knees, he's able to coast into second.

* * *

Guessing how he got on the staff is easy enough, but why is more interesting. I don't think it was all about my development, which is all he would ever admit to. I think it has a lot to do with what went on during my eighth grade year when I didn't play. Dad didn't like me not playing, and he obviously didn't like me hanging around that hobby shop. When he yelled at me about girls, he knew what he was doing.

I was tall for my age and I guess I was nice looking as far as girls were concerned. My hair the right shade of brown. My eyes blue. They started paying attention to me really early. Every once in a while, if I was out somewhere with friends or by myself, I'd see a high school girl who didn't know who I was looking over at me. I was too shy to do anything about it with older girls, but I had awkward middle school relationships with a good part of my class before we ever got to high school.

Both my parents knew, of course, and they didn't mind, though Mom took a little persuading to be convinced that I should be left alone. Parents never realize how much kids are able to figure out from snippets of conversation, and I overheard the words "he" and "girls" enough to know that Mom thought I was spending too much mental energy deciding who I thought was the cutest while Dad insisted that if that were the case, he'd see it on the field, and he hadn't seen it on the field, so it just showed that I was a good-looking boy. "He'd better get used to the attention. It's going to get more intense if he makes it."

At this point, Mom would start in about how he was counting my chickens, and Dad would insist that he knew the odds were not in my favor, but that it was a real possibility because I was special. They were both right.

* * *

Everyone in the dugout is standing. Everyone in the stadium is standing. The bullpen is going because the other manager knows this might get out of hand in a hurry. Brian walks to the plate and seeing him just now is like seeing him three or four years ago when there had only been a couple of knee surgeries. It must be a mirage, this grace and youth in his step, but I swear I see it.

Just like Dave, Brian doesn't take the bat off his shoulder as the first pitch goes by. Doesn't even twitch. He watches. Ball. Strike. Strike. Ball. Ball. It's a full count and we've solved something, you can see it. The next pitch comes in, and Brian loads his swing and hits a sharp line drive toward left. Ramirez dives and almost catches it, but he doesn't. The ball goes off the end of his glove and skitters into no-man's land. First and third. No outs. The stadium is shaking. Cups of Gatorade tremble all over the dugout. A loose ball rolls to the ground. And here's Carver.

* * *

Girls weren't anything to be worried about. I liked the attention, but I didn't know what to do about it. Then eighth grade happened. I really did take the year off because I was tired of baseball and because I was sick of Dad pushing me so hard, but that doesn't mean I didn't have second thoughts. Taking the year off meant I got to see my gaming friends more, but it meant I hardly saw my baseball friends at all. A lot of them were pissed at me, too. They knew I was the best pitcher around, and they knew they'd lose more games without me on the team.

The importance of sacrificing for the team gets drilled in very early when you play sports. By eighth grade, my friends knew the language well enough, and I heard all the clichés. "You're really letting us down, Zack." "What about the team?" "We were depending on you to help us." Having been indoctrinated just as they had, I thought they had a very good point. Now I'd tell them that no one cares about what an eighth-grade baseball team does and that it's much more important at that age to figure out who you are and who you want to be than to worry about commitment to something you might not enjoy anymore. But, at the time, it was really hard.

I was on the point of breaking—the season hadn't started yet, and there was still plenty of time to sign up—when I met Ashley.

Ashley was one grade behind me, but we went to the same school, so it was surprising I'd never noticed her before. It was more surprising because I learned that she spent almost as much time in the hobby shop as I did. Somehow, our paths just hadn't crossed.

* * *

Carver is up now. I don't like Carver, but I don't hate him either, and I am on my feet just like everyone else hoping the little weasel can get something done. He's not like Brian and Dave, though. He can't sit still. He fouls the first pitch off. Whoever is down in the bullpen is moving fast. Carver fouls off the second pitch. He takes a ball. He's guessing. He doesn't know what's coming like Dave and Brian did. He doesn't see what they saw.

The next pitch comes and he hits a one-hopper right to Ramirez. The double play happens so quickly Dave can't even think about going home. He's stuck on third and it's still tied, but now there are two outs. The pitcher in the bullpen sits back down. The stadium is quiet. Manny comes up.

* * *

Ashley was Dad's worst nightmare. She wore a lot of black clothes except when she went out dressed like one of her favorite characters, her hair color changed from week to week, and she didn't like being outside when she could be inside watching the newest episode of whatever it was or playing Magic or Dungeons and Dragons. At thirteen, I thought she was as magical as she wanted to be.

First, we have to remember that I was very thirteen. What really appealed to me initially about Ashley was that she had, to put it delicately, developed significantly more than most of the other girls I was around, and that she liked some of the same things I did. It was unusual to find girls who cared about gaming back then. I would imagine that I held similar appeal. Not that it was hard to find boys, but I was definitely different from most of the boys who spent time around the hobby shop.

Superficial as our attraction was, at the time, we both thought we were soul mates. I remember a lot of talk about how perfectly matched we were and how lucky we were to have found each other already. "It's so nice to really know already, you know? To know for sure. It's so freeing." I remember her saying this, but I might have said it. We were equally stupid. I'm not trying to place myself on a pedestal.

We weren't perfect for each other, either. Not only did Ashley not like being outside, she hated sports in general and baseball especially. "It's soooo boring. Nothing happens." That was definitely her.

I should have known to run the other way, but instead, I did what so many kids do and assumed that the opinions of the person I liked should be my opinions, too. Though, once again in the interest of being fair, I believe I cost her a season of a couple of her favorite shows that I declared, loudly, to be "stupid kid shows."

Eventually, I would wise up, and in a different era, my parents never would have known how serious we were. I wasn't intentionally forthcoming with any information, but I didn't have a cell phone yet. They were still new and pretty expensive, and neither of my parents could see the use. Ashley didn't have one either, which meant that all of our meetings had to be set up from our home phones. Later, when things began to heat up to a point that might have alarmed our parents, we'd send notes through friends.

Seeing me talk to a girl wasn't an odd experience, but seeing me talk to the same girl for several months was. Mom was the first one who pieced together that there might be a little more going on than either of them had seen.

"So, you and Ashley seem to like each other a lot."

"Yeah, she's cool."

"You see her down at the game shop, right?"

Here I would shrug my shoulders in a vague attempt to make our encounters seem unimportant. "I guess so."

"Is there anything we need to talk about with that?"

Since the dawn of time, sentences like those have signaled to kids that their parents might want to talk to them about sex. I would have perked up and said whatever I needed to get myself out of there. I probably could have used a bit of a talk at that time, actually, but I sure wasn't going to say anything to Mom about it, if I could help it.

It was maybe a week after that conversation when Dad showed up at the hobby shop. This was strange for a lot of reasons, not the least of which was that my dad hated that place and never set foot in it if he could help it. I can't remember what his trumped-up excuse was for coming to find me instead of calling the store and telling me to come home, which is what he normally did, but it was very apparent that his real reason was to see Ashley. He talked to her a lot more than he talked to me. I was disgusted by his behavior, and I wasn't shy about letting everyone know it when he left.

"Stupid old man. Why can't he just respect me?" This with my best adolescent puffery.

If I was mad then, I was furious when I got home and had to listen to Dad's opinion of Ashley over dinner.

"Why don't you want to hang out with normal girls?" Then he looked at my mom. "Orange, Steph. Her hair was orange."

"Well she sounds perfectly nice to me. I don't know if I'd want my hair to be orange, but she can have hers however she wants it."

Mom had her concerns about the relationship, but she also wanted me to know that she thought my dad was full of it. She couldn't fight both battles at once, so she picked a side.

* * *

Something is happening that pops me out of my memory. It takes me a minute to find out what it is. I don't know how long I drifted off for, but Manny is still at bat. The scoreboard says there's a full count. I see him foul off a pitch. And then another. And then another. The crowd gets louder the longer the at bat goes. Another foul. Guillen doesn't want to walk Manny, but he doesn't want to give him a pitch he can handle. Manny is trying to stay alive.

Another foul. Each time Manny makes contact, a cheer goes up.

The next pitch is perfect. a curveball that the bottom drops right out of. Somehow, Manny gets underneath it just enough to get it into the air, but not high into the air. I see Newhall, the second baseman, jump, but it's over his head, and even though the outfielders are playing in, neither of them can get to it. Dave, who was off with the pitch, trots home. We all scream and point to Manny, who points back, waves to the crowd and starts bouncing around first. We are winning.

* * *

I spent a couple of months deriding baseball before I couldn't take it anymore. I might not have wanted to play that year, but that didn't mean I was totally ready to cast it aside. I see now that Mom and Dad both had come over to the same side and were working together. Baseball was on the TV all the time and dad mentioned one night, when he caught me peeking at the game, that he thought I might like to go down to Louisville for a game soon. "It's been a while since we've been down there. We can eat at that spaghetti place you like."

"What about Kristen?"

"Oh, she'll come, too. And Mom. Hell, maybe we'll make a weekend of it and go to a couple of games."

This was a big expenditure for us. We didn't just take weekend trips, and to thirteen-year-old me, it sounded awesome. Two baseball games in a weekend and food I wanted to eat. I couldn't really ask for anything more. He broke me.

When I told Ashley about it, she was indignant. "You're going to be gone the whole weekend to watch some stupid baseball games? I thought you didn't even like that stuff anymore."

"I still like to watch games. I'm just not sure I want to play."

I remember she gave me an exasperated look and rolled her eyes at me and then we went back to normal. She was pretty cold for a while after that. It's funny the stupid stuff that matters when you're that age. I play baseball for a living now, and I don't think I'll care if I end up married to someone who doesn't like it. That might be nice given how all-encompassing it can be.

It was the beginning of the end for Ashley and me. Mom and Dad knew exactly how to handle things. They even made a point of stopping by some of the gaming shops in Louisville, which were much bigger than what we had. I could see that dad thought it was stupid, but the gesture mattered. And it was hard not to get back to loving baseball after that.

* * *

Guillen is drenched with sweat. The crowd is bouncing. The bullpen is busy again, and Adam settles in. There are times in a baseball game where the outs are more surprising than the hits. That should never be the case. Even a great hitter against a mediocre pitcher is at a disadvantage. Guillen is good. He wins more than he loses. This year, his ERA was 3.10. Even tired and against the ropes as he is now, he shouldn't be taken for granted.

Adam knows this. Others on the team might not, but Adam does. His approach harkens back to the way Dave and Brian handled Guillen, but somehow, it seems to Guillen's advantage to slow things down. You can see him regain control of his emotions. He gets ahead of Adam one ball and two strikes. The crowd is happy, but they don't want to see the inning end.

Then Adam does what he does best. He swings flat and hard and true and sends a rope into right-center. Manny is running hard. He's around second and heading to third, and he's being waved in, but he doesn't look at the coach. He hits the third base bag and throws himself to the left, the perfect turn. Martin has the ball and unleashes an insane throw that comes into home on the fly. Ferris grabs it and brings the tag around. It's close, but it's not a photo finish. Manny is in, foot across the plate before Ferris has turned all the way.

* * *

That trip is what got me back on the path. On the drive back home, I made some comment about a pitcher we'd seen who was supposed to be the next big thing. Dad pounced. "You could do that, you know. If you decided you wanted to play again."

I fidgeted in my seat.

"Are you telling me you haven't been missing it?"

"Maybe a little."

"High school, too. The games get bigger there. You can play in tournaments. It won't be like the basketball team, but still, it might be nice."

He couldn't be as direct with Mom in the car, but I knew what he was implying. Lots of girls paying attention. They both knew I hadn't been talking to Ashley as much on the phone. The idea of more girls was getting more appealing by the day.

Mom and Dad sat in silence in the front of the car for a while and let me stew, then Mom chimed in. "You know, Zack. I know you love baseball. Just because some people don't doesn't mean you have to give it up. Do what makes you happy. You don't have to play if you don't want to, but don't let others tell you what you want."

That's such a mom thing to say, but she said it and it worked, which is probably why moms say that kind of stuff all the time.

"I might like to play this year." Dad got so excited he swerved into the other lane for a second, but no one said anything. Except Mom, who reminded me that I could play card games and baseball, which was very Mom.

* * *

The manager comes out and talks to Guillen. I can see from Guillen's expression that he wants to stay in. It's only the fourth, he's saying. It's early. If it were me out there, I'd already be gone. We lost the first game. Jerry's not going to let this one get out of hand. But they have some padding. Taking Guillen out now could screw the bullpen up a little, even with the off day tomorrow. Anyone close enough to see can lip read what the manager says. "You've got one more batter."

* * *

Ashley and I called it quits as soon as I told her I was going to play again. I'm really giving this silly middle school relationship more thought than it deserves, but it was a turning point. Dad finagled the coaching spot because he wanted to keep an eye on me. Mom let him because she wanted an eye kept on me. I probably had gotten a little too serious about Ashley, which Mom didn't like, and Ashley'd almost kept me out of baseball, which Dad didn't like.

And so Dad was around as much as he could be. More than he had been. But he wasn't so much of a jerk. He had his moments, but he didn't want to lose me or my potential career. It was still weird. It

would always be weird, the way Dad was so invested in my pitching, but for a while, I didn't mind it.

* * *

Matt comes up, Adam is on second, and Guillen
is giving home plate the death stare. His fastball
gets up to only ninety-two, but it moves. The first
one gets by Matt for a strike. The next pitch is a
curve that drops in for a strike. Matt smartly sits
tight for the next two pitches, both balls, but then
he pops another curveball up behind the plate.
Ferris grabs it. Guillen is still in the game, but he's
not winning any more.

Top of the Fifth.

When we take the field in the top of the inning, all of us stand straight. We bounce and prance like ebullient race horses. We aren't trying to show up the other team, but it's hard to contain after what just happened. We're winning, we look in control. Why not be happy for a moment?

It's funny how little joy you're supposed to show as a baseball player. If I strike out Ferris, I'm not really allowed to pump my fist or shout. Unless maybe it kills a rally at the end of an inning. And even then, I can't overdo it. As though Mike Ferris doesn't understand that. Doesn't know how good he is and that it's a victory worth celebrating when a pitcher beats him. We are always told how lucky we are that we play a children's game every day, and then we are derided if ever we act like children. The world is contradictory.

But what we do right now breaks no unwritten rules. We are allowed to look happy when winning a World Series game at home against a very good team. We are allowed to bounce a little.

I finish my warm-up pitches, and they are so easy, and I feel so good, that I am reminded of when Dad told me I'd be great. I was a sophomore in high school when he told me. He didn't equivocate. It wasn't that I could be great. It wasn't that I'd be great if I applied myself. I would be great he insisted. I asked how he could be so sure.

"Because," he said, "no one has to pay any attention to you in the middle innings."

"Huh?"

"You tire out eventually, like everyone does, and sometimes in the first, you take a minute to find your spot. But they have to get you early or late. There's nothing they can do in the middle."

This was something Dad had harped on about pitchers for as long as I can remember. I don't know if it's true or not, but he always insisted the best pitchers were the ones who made you think that if you didn't get to them right away, there would be no getting to them at all. How great they were was all about how often it was possible to get to them early. In high school, I lost my control a lot, but he was right: If nothing happened in the first, that was it. Any runs that came in were a product of luck. It's not something that's changed as I've grown up.

We are in the exact middle of the game now, though I am a bit past my middle point. I won't finish the game—too many pitches—but I'm hoping to make it through the seventh, at least. In any case, I am untouchable right now.

I'm still in the bottom of the order. Togneri-Jones is up. Last time, he sneaked on. This time, I think I've got him when he send a slider bouncing toward Adam. It looks like an easy enough play. Routine. And then the kind of thing happens that none of us has any control over. The ball hits something—a hard clump of dirt, a little divot—and it kicks to Adam's right. He gets his glove on it, but doesn't hold on. He picks it up and makes a throw, but Togneri-Jones is on again. Easy innings are hard to come by tonight.

Fortunately for me, they send Newhall up with orders to bunt. He does just as they ask, but it dies right in front of Brian, who pounces on it and sends it to Adam at second before he relays it to Alex at first. Two outs.

And Ramirez is coming up.

Ramirez versus me is the real contest of this game and everyone in the park knows it. It was made clear when I wet my pants in the first inning and he took advantage the way everyone expected him to. Twice he has led off an inning. Twice he has reached and scored, but this situation is different.

This time, I am not scared. I am in a groove. I am pitching well. My team is winning. Still, we must take him seriously.

He steps in with his piston bounce. Brian calls for a fastball, and as I reach back to throw it as hard as I can, his body stills. He does not flinch as the pitch misses just inside for ball one. Brian calls for a fastball again. Same location. He bounces. I reach back. He stills. Does not flinch. This time, I am better. Strike one. The stadium is quiet. If he reaches, nothing important will change, but it will feel like we are losing. We will have surrendered something. I will have surrendered something. I will have shown that I cannot beat him. If they can extend the game, send him to the plate enough times, he will beat us. By himself if he has to. I think of how Dad would be at moments like this. How he would breathe only between pitches. As soon as I came set before the pitch, he would hold his breath. Wait.

It wasn't intentional. I never told him I noticed it. I don't know if he still did it. I don't know if he did it when he watched me a few days ago. It's been ages since he sat close enough for me to tell. Brian calls for a change-up. Ramirez gets out in front of it and sends it foul. One ball. Two strikes. We are winning the battle. Brian calls for a slider, hoping to finish him. Ramirez bounces. Stills. Doesn't bite. Ball two. Another slider is called. It doesn't find the zone either. The count is full. The stadium is still dead silent. No one moves. No one breathes.

It is as though my dad is somehow filling every seat in the stadium. Brian calls fastball. It's a good pitch. A great pitch. But it doesn't quite finish the job. Ramirez fouls it off. I can feel everyone shifting nervously in their seats. A glance in the dugout finds everyone standing and silent. Brian wants a fastball again. I give it to him and Ramirez does something insane. He bunts.

Ramirez is a good hitter. He's fast enough to bunt for a hit, but he doesn't have to. Bunting now makes no sense. A foul bunt with two strikes and he's out—the inning is over. He's relying on this. He must be. He wants to create chaos. He wants to catch us unaware, and he does. It's a good bunt, off into no-man's land between home, third, and the mound. It's my play, and I have to move quickly, but it's just a force play. If I get the ball there first, I win. It's an awkward move, no matter how I approach it, to pick up the ball, turn, and throw. I eschew my glove and barehand the ball successfully. I turn, whip the ball hard toward first, and fall over. As I fall, I don't allow my head to turn. I keep my eyes fixed on Alex at first. I see Ramirez flying down the line. I see the ball pop into Alex's glove. I hear the thump of a Ramirez's foot on the bag. I feel the my hip and shoulder collide softly with the turf. I see the fist pumping out call of the umpire. I hear Ramirez shout and shake his fist in defeat. I smell the grass. I hear the crowd scream. I hear the crowd scream. I hear the crowd scream. I stand. I feel Manny slap my butt as he runs past me to the dugout. Ramirez cuts across the field and as he passes me, he nods. Touches his cap just for a moment.

Bottom of the Fifth.

The cheers of the crowd come down like a thunderstorm. The stadium rumbles. The ground shakes. It takes me just a moment to remember that I am supposed to run back to the dugout. When I get there and sit down, I close my eyes and listen to the downpour. If it was real and the heavens had opened up like this, the game would be over. It is the bottom of the fifth and we are winning. If the game were called, it would be over. I could say, "I did it, Dad. I won a World Series game. I won. Five innings. Two runs. That's not bad. I did it, Dad. I did it."

If I could say that. If I could say it and be heard. If I could.

But the downpour slows to a patter. I open my eyes. Remember. A clear night. The moon rising now, not quite full. More game to be played. Russell Jennings coming to bat.

* * *

Watching the media circus around Russell this year was something. Our fans were, of course, immediately supportive. After all, he had just led the league in OPS. He had finished an unfair second in the MVP vote. Can't boo that guy. We started at home this year and when his name was announced, he got the biggest cheer of anyone. Even bigger than me, and I'd *won* the Cy Young and hadn't been accused of any violent crimes.

Of course, I am quiet and not a good quote. The reason Russell got such a cheer is that he handled the media and the fans like he handles the bat. He gave an interview a few days before Opening Day that was calculated to give him exactly that kind of ovation. I still have the article saved on my phone. I look at it when I want to feel bad, I guess.

Do you have anything to say about the ongoing allegations?

Well, my lawyers are going to be really mad at me for this—I haven't warned them or anything—but it's time to tell the truth. The truth is, yes, she was in my room. Everybody knows that already, there's no use denying it, and I don't like lying. But I didn't do anything wrong.

What happened then?

Oh come on, now. I don't want to drag the girl's reputation through the dirt.

But just saying she was in your room...

There's going to be a lot of he said, she said. The only people who will ever know what happened are the two of us. We've been fully cooperating with the police, as they'll tell you (ed. Local police confirm that Jennings has made himself readily available). I didn't do anything wrong. I let a pretty girl come up to my room. I learned later, I don't know if I'm supposed to talk about this, but I learned she's had some problems. I wish we could help her out. But now, it would look like something it wasn't.

That's going to read as pandering, you realize?

So what if it does? The truth reads like a lie sometimes, doesn't it? Look at how I present myself. Talk to the people around me. Talk to my teammates. This isn't the kind of person I am. I don't do things like this. I like to go out, I like to have fun, but I don't want to hurt anybody. I have women in my life. My mom, my sisters. I'm not going to do anything to hurt a woman. I was raised better than that.

It went on from there. I don't find it particularly convincing, frankly, but I guess it could be, if you were already looking for a reason to be convinced. I think the reporter should be fired, though. He was making it much too easy. But then, Russell is too smart to do anything uncalculated. He knew the reporter was friendly. There's a reason he picked a national writer and not one of the local guys. I bet his lawyers knew what was up, too.

* * *

The roar is just as loud today as it was on that first day. The crowd can't stop cheering him. I have no need, though. Let him strike out. Let him look silly. I don't care. We're winning. There's nothing he can do for me right now.

Guillen looks focused. He's on a short leash and he knows it. The bullpen hasn't quieted all the way. Two guys are out there tossing gently, staying loose in case they have to get ready in a hurry.

He starts off with a fastball and Russell watches it go by. Three more pitches and Russell still hasn't taken the bat off his shoulder, and he's ahead three balls and a strike. They're scared of him. They go ahead and make the fourth ball intentional and the crowd goes off. It's the World Series and they want to see him hit. They love him and they know he gives them a chance to win. But no one wants to risk grooving a pitch to him, so down to first he goes amid a shower of boos. If the boos were meant for him, the world would be a little more just.

* * *

When the season started, Russell would get some boos on the road. He'd get some signs expressing displeasure, but he always knew how to handle it. He'd get questions from the local media and feign earnest frustration. *It's hard, man. What am I supposed to say? When someone commits a crime, you expect them to deny it. When they don't, you expect them to deny it. There's no evidence I can put forth. I just have to rely on my character. People know me. I feel like the fans know me, and they believe me. I have to rely on that. I'm just glad I've lived my life so that people will believe me.*

Russell has always been about his public image. Most all of us give to charity, of course. I mean, if you make as much money as we do and don't give some of it away, people give you dirty looks. I think that's fair. I don't make a big deal about the money I give out. Some do. Some like to be out working with people. Sometimes just because they want to help and sometimes because they want to be seen as helping. I probably should be a little more public, but I don't want to be, so I'm not. I don't think it makes me better than the next guy or anything. I'm just chicken is all.

Russell's always been about shaking hands. He gives away enough money that no one can complain, and he's always public about it. He has these little projects that he supposedly runs, but really, he just shows up for photo ops and does what his people tell him to do. He could be a politician if he wanted. He'll be one of those players who retires into a nice TV contract. He'll play it right, and he'll be the kind of guy who gets to break juicy little tidbits. And if he keeps up like he is, he'll get into the Hall, and that's only going to boost his credentials.

I was really sick about it for a while. A few of us talked about it. Those of us in the rotation all stick pretty close and we get along well. Joel is our number two, and I think he was the first one who said something, actually. It's a coincidence that we all have sisters. Having sisters helps, I think. Though it shouldn't be necessary, and obviously, as you can tell from Russell, it doesn't always get the job done. Joel said something about not wanting to see Russell anywhere near his sister. We all agreed, though generally, our sisters have been around long enough that they don't have interest in ballplayers.

So we all talked about it for a while and some-body brought up the idea of leaking things to the press. I thought it might be a good idea, and I called Dad about it.

"Won't do any good."

"Why not. People should know. He's getting cheers everywhere."

"He's getting cheers because he's being upfront—pretending to be upfront—in every city. Some little bit leaks out and it just reads like sour grapes. Some other player on the team who doesn't like the attention Russell's getting. You want to get him, you'd have to go on the record."

"What if someone did?"

"They'd lose a lot of money on their next contract I bet. And Russell'd denounce them, which would count for a lot since he's so good. Lot of boos at home for that player."

I didn't say anything.

"You could maybe do it. You're good enough. You've got hardware and Russell doesn't. You're having just as good a year as he is, so no sour grapes. Still, the fans wouldn't like it. And you're about to be a free agent."

"Do you think it would make a difference?"

"It's not putting him in jail. I can tell you that. Might mess up the season for you guys, though."

Having this piece of knowledge and not know-ing what to do with it is hard. I wasn't happy with what Dad told me, so I called Kristen and asked what she thought. I kind of knew what she'd say.

"He said *what*? And the prosecutor's office reacted *how*? Zack! How have you not said anything? You have to tell somebody."

"But do you think it will do any good?"

"Will it do any good? Zack!" She was livid. When she said my name, she stretched it into two syllables so she could squeeze in all her exasperation. *Za-ack!*

"It's just, I was talking to Dad."

"Oh yeah, Dad. I think we all know what Dad would have to say about that."

"Well, actually, he said I was probably the only one on the team who could do it."

"Did he encourage you?"

"I don't know. Maybe."

"Uh huh."

"Kristen, come on."

"Zack, do you have any idea how many of these guys are out there? And they all think they can do it because everyone turns a blind eye."

She was right. I knew she was right. You can't really argue with someone when they are so clearly right, so I shut up and let her lecture me and let her make me feel terrible and then, I guess because she's my sister and she loves me, she said this:

"Zack, I understand if you don't say anything. Dad's right. It probably won't do any good. I'd like you to say something. I'd like someone to call him out. Someone should. But I get that it won't matter. That it might mess things up for you. I get it."

I went back after that and talked to the other guys in the rotation. It came up over and over for a while when different guys told their sisters about it, but eventually it just faded into the background. Something we put up with. Our sisters all said they understood or had no reaction. None of us ever said anything, on the record or off. I wonder if we understood.

* * *

Alex is up now. I have a feeling that Guillen is running on fumes. I'd like to see things get out of hand for him quickly, but you never know in baseball. Alex gets deep in the count, too, and ends up with a full count. This is good for us. Guillen is going to be lucky to get out of this inning. Alex doesn't quite get it done, though. He hits a big, deep fly ball. In the heat of August, it probably goes over the wall. But now, in the cold, it drops just in front for the first out of the inning. Still, the bullpen is working.

* * *

When I talked to Dad about Russell, it was just as impossible as it always was to figure out what he actually thought. I think what he said was true. I don't think anything I could have done would have sent Russell to jail. I think, all things being equal, that he'd have been happy to see Russell get what he deserves. But then, why mention that saying something would cost me money?

We talked about it a few more times throughout the season, and every time he gave the same impression. It would be "right" to say something, but it would do more harm than good, so what would the point be? I came to feel like I was being manipulated. Effectively manipulated, I guess, since I'm sitting in the dugout at the very, very end of the season and still haven't said anything.

Dad and I got along a lot better when I was in high school, but looking back, it's been hard to wonder if it wasn't just a change in his approach. When I'd been smaller, he'd been willing to bully me to get what he wanted out of me. That's what the sparrow speech started as. But in high school, it was different. There was the coaching thing, for one, but around the house he was a lot different.

I was a star on the team right away, and that came with some ego. Dad wasn't going to try to take me head on anymore, though. Sometimes, I'd be sore or tired or just lazy and there was no way in the world I was going to work out unless it was a team practice. The first time it happened I was sitting in my room playing video games when Dad walked past and then stuck his head in.

"You get up early today?"

"No."

"Shouldn't you be doing the morning workout, then?"

"Too sore today." I didn't even look at him. I was focused on my game, and I didn't want to make eye contact if I could help it.

"Huh. Looked nice out. I'll have to look again. Thought I heard a sparrow out there. Must be wrong." And then he walked away.

I sat there for a few minutes, trying to focus on the game, but he'd gotten himself into my head, so I hit save, turned it off, and went outside to work out. It was a nice day. There were birds everywhere.

* * *

Now Hector. Ferris walks out to the mound to discuss how they want to approach Hector. That didn't happen at the beginning of the season, but as he's come on, teams have gotten more cautious with him. Whatever their plan is, it doesn't work, even if they do get the out. Guillen throws a curveball that doesn't break and Hector hits a hard, straight line drive the rattles against the wall in left center. Russell moves quick and is waved in, but Coates has an arm and this throw is every bit as hard coming back as the hit was going out. They get Russell at the plate. Maybe I chuckle a little. Can't say.

The manager comes out and there's a pretty good discussion out there on the mound. You can tell Guillen doesn't want to come out. It would be humiliating to come out of a World Series game in the fifth inning, but it's also pretty clear he doesn't have much left. He's lucky the score isn't more lopsided than it is. Managers like the idea of a pitcher finishing an inning, though. And I guess they aren't quite as afraid of Dave as the guys coming before him. That's fair. Dave can be beat if you change speeds on him, and Guillen's good at that.

* * *

After that first time, it wasn't long until the whole sparrow thing became a point of affection between us. It was a way for him to call me out without directly challenging me, which would never have worked. "Raining a little, but the sparrows are still at the feeder." "Cold out today. Did you see how hungry the birds are?" Sometimes, I'd still blow him off, but most of the time, I'd roll off my bed or out from in front of the TV and go work out.

Dad's other big tactic at the time was to find video of top prospects and show it to me. "See this guy. 95. Decent curveball. Control issues."

"I have control issues."

"This guy just got drafted in the second round by the Mets."

"Huh."

That's a hard feeling to articulate—being fifteen or sixteen years old and seeing players who are supposed to be in the majors in a few years and thinking, *well, I can pretty much do that.*

No scouts were paying attention to me, though. We were in the middle of nowhere in Indiana. Small high school. Good, but not great. I'd get some looks later, of course, but as a sophomore, I wasn't on the radar yet.

* * *

Dave steps in. One way or another, I have to believe this is it for Guillen. If he gets the out, he finishes with five innings. Not great, but not a disgrace. If Dave gets on, Guillen gets yanked. I've always hated getting yanked. That's Dad's fault as much as anything else I do. Dad had a weird tick about pitchers who couldn't get out of the inning when they ran into trouble. He had an even bigger thing about managers sending a tired pitcher back out. He used to swear at the TV over it. He'd go on and on about how this or that pitcher better call a surgeon. Most of it had to do with Dad's sense of order. He liked clean innings. He liked clean games.

* * *

"He takes the sharpness out of games now." This was what Dad said to me after a few months of watching Russell this season. "All the fans screaming for him or against him. It interrupts the flow."

"No one really boos him now, Dad."

"My point stands. He's a spectacle. Never be a spectacle, Zack."

"I know, Dad."

Never be a spectacle. I don't know when this became Dad's philosophy. But he sure held to it. That's why he hated a pitcher coming out. He said it was a spectacle. The manager coming out to fetch him like a parent busting a pot-smoking teenager.

"It's humiliating. You have to see it coming. Managers don't pay enough attention and they're greedy. They always want more. It's a spectacle."

My dad knew a lot about baseball, but he never understood this. He thought he could see it because it's always easy to see things in hindsight, but I've been on the mound a lot more than he has. I won the Cy Young Award last year. I know about pitching. I know that sometimes you feel fine and then the next pitch, it's gone. That sudden. It can be in the middle of an inning or the middle of a batter. Sometimes you tire slowly. Sometimes you don't.

* * *

Guillen should be out, though. He's spent. Dad would be screaming furiously at the TV right now. He would hate what's going on. I can hear it. "They've had the bullpen up half the night. Use the pen! That's what you have them for." The last sentence he'd almost sing, his voice rising in the condescending way of a parent who has watched his child make the same stupid mistake over and over again.

But no. The manager is being greedy. He wants one more out. He wants his first reliever to start the sixth out fresh.

Guillen starts with a fastball and it's just a mess. He's dropping his arm and he's losing velocity. If the ball had been anywhere near the plate, we'd have two more runs now. Ferris can see it, I'm sure. Guillen probably can, too. The next pitch is a curve. Guillen still has his curve. He'll probably be able to break that pitch off when he has grandkids. It drops through the strike zone and Dave watches it for a strike. The next pitch is another curveball that Dave fouls off. The crowd is pretty pumped up. They want Dave to hit one out. Four runs feels like it would be too much for the other team. The game would be as good as won. Like my dad, they don't understand how fast it can turn.

* * *

The sparrow thing never left us, but it changed a little. Later in high school, when scouts were looking and Dad didn't have to make me work out, it was something he'd yell out at the mound when I was starting to lose it mentally. "Sparrow dancing around here by the bleachers, Zack, time to work." Sometimes it worked and sometimes it didn't. It was like a mini-mound conference where Dad told me to stop thinking so much. Just work. Pitching was an art. Work was work. Don't be an artist.

Follow directions. Do as I was told. Dad knew me well enough to know this was a good strategy with me. Sometimes, I just lost it, and there was nothing anyone could do. But Dad helped the most.

* * *

Guillen has lost it, but that doesn't always matter. Dave gets on top of a curveball and sends a sharp little grounder to Ramirez. Not that it matters how hard it's hit. A ball would have to levitate above the infielder for Dave to beat out anything. The inning is over.

It's silly, but as I grab my glove and jog out to get ready for the sixth, I look around the park. You see birds sometimes. They come after the discarded food. The hotdog buns and popcorn. I can't usually tell what they are, but sometimes I notice a sparrow. I know all the sparrows. I'm looking for one now, but I don't see anything. I sure would love to see a sparrow, but there are no sparrows. Just the crowd.

Top of the Sixth.

Baseball would fit right into Ecclesiastes. The season beginneth and the season endeth and in the spring, the season beginneth again. Each game does also beginneth and endeth. So too each inning with the coming and going of six outs. And each out and each pitch doth beginneth and endeth.

Or something like that.

There is a rhythm to the game. Everything does feel like a cycle. It doesn't take long until every game situation feels like something you've already seen. Though it will surprise you sometimes, the only thing that changes about the game is how you deal with it.

And so the sixth starts and again I am on the mound throwing warm-up pitches. I am not letting myself look for sparrows. I am not letting myself look. I can't lay that extra baggage on myself right now. In the cycle of the game, the sixth is where I usually start to feel a little tense. A little nervous. More than half of the game is done. We're winning or we're losing. I can feel the day's pitches in my arm. Especially if many of them have been thrown under pressure.

We're still winning, and this is starting to look like a good game for me. Five innings, two runs. If I add another inning or two, people will look back and say I did my job. I like doing my job. I'm not someone who dwells on my own performance more than the team's. I want to win. I always want to win, but there is satisfaction in pitching well and losing. Everyone gets beat sometimes. Even on good days. It's what I like about baseball. Not so much separates the best of us from the worst of us. A guy who can barely hold on might throw as hard as me. Might throw the same pitches, but maybe his slider moves a little less and so hitters see it a little better and maybe his change-up is a little easier to read. I'm not so different from that guy.

Except, of course, that I'm here and he's not. It's a thin line. And here is Xavier Coates. This is the third time around, but the first time I've been concerned with him. There are no easy batters now. Not at this point. Not with the game close. Brian and I also know that this is likely the last time I will face Coates. We don't need to hold anything back, so we don't. He fights well. He works a full count. Fouls a couple of pitches off, but in the end, he misses a slider and I get to move to the next batter.

Mike Ferris steps in and shows that sometimes there's nothing you can do. I throw a pitch exactly where I want it. He guesses exactly right. A line drive heads out to left-center and Ferris coasts into second. One pitch. That's all I got against him. I look at him and shake my head. I look at Brian and shrug. The next three batters are all dangerous. They could all make it a tie game if they get under one. So now, it is very serious.

Martin steps up and, for what must be the thousandth time, the crowd is silent. Playoff crowds and regular season crowds are different. If this were July, the level of attention would have increased with Ferris' double, but people would still be trucking off to the bathroom or to get another beer. It wouldn't be world-stopping. If Martin knocks one and ties the game, that's a shame, but, hey, it's July. Different now. Different in October. The season beginneth and the season endeth and we are in no hurry for the endeth. Not now.

I feel it, too. Of course I do. Some guys try to deny it. Try to pretend that every game is the same. I wish I could do that, but I can't. I try to find the groove. I try to keep things familiar, but the tension is real. The pressure is real. It's the World Series.

I'll miss Dad in the regular season. I know I will. But I wish he was here right now. I wish Mom and Kristen were, too. But I have Brian, at least. I can listen to him. I can see that he feels like I do. Even behind the mask.

I get lost in this. The people who are missing. The people who are here. I follow directions, but I don't pay attention to anything else. I know the at-bat with Martin starts to stretch and I come to when the count is full. I miss and I walk him and for some reason, this brings a wave of sadness over me and it is all I can do not to start crying on the mound. Dad wouldn't care. He knows that walks happen. I've had it together since the first, mostly. But what if I don't now?

But I am so sad. Brian sees that something is wrong. He calls time and comes out.

"What's up, man?"

"I don't know."

"Hey, it's fine. We'll get out of it."

"I know. I know. It's just—" I can hardly hold the tears back and I have to stop talking. I don't even know what I'm thinking about that's making this happen, but it's happening.

"This sucks. You know?" Brian says.

I look up at him and his face is dead serious.

"Your dad should be out there somewhere. The way it happened. It's enough to make you doubt everything."

I do not know why he has chosen this moment to have this conversation. On the mound doesn't seem the right place. But it's perfect, too. So much of our friendship has happened on the field. He reaches out and puts his gloved left hand on my shoulder.

"It doesn't matter now, you know. You've done enough. No one would blame you losing it right now. Whatever else you do is nothing."

"I'm not ready to come out yet." I'm starting to get hold of myself again.

"No. I know. Come on, then. Two more."

He turns around and trots back to the plate. I throw a pitch. Apolinar pops it up. It wasn't a good pitch, but he missed and Alex camps under it. Two on with two outs is a lot different than two on with one out. I feel like there should be some kind of life metaphor in that, but I can't think of one. And here is Takeda.

With two outs and the crowd relaxing, something about what Brian said starts to sink in. I know that it doesn't matter. I have pitched almost six innings in a World Series game four days after my dad died. I have done my duty. I have had moments of uncertainty, but I have done well. Everyone will praise me. If I strike out Takeda, they will cheer loudly and I will tip my cap and they will scream and the press interviews will be reverent. If he hits a home run and we lose the lead, the stadium will be mournful, but they will still applaud me when Jerry comes out to get me. I will not tip my cap, but I may touch the bill as I near the dugout. I will have been one pitch away from a good start four days after my dad died and no one will say anything bad. They will be amazed that I was able to come so close because anyone who has thought about it knows. They know that such a loss at such a moment is unthinkable. They know that it is wrong that I have been deprived of my grief. That I have been forced to grieve here in front of them all. There is nothing I can do to hurt myself right now. It is only a matter of how much I want. I want more.

And the first pitch to Takeda is a strike. And the second pitch to Takeda is a ball. Foul. Foul. Ball. Foul. He is stubborn, but it does not matter because I cannot lose. I throw another pitch and it is a ball and the count is full for the second time this inning. And then another pitch and he connects and it sounds loud and scary, but the angle is not right. It's too high in the air. It is loud, but unspectacular. Hector needs only a short, thunderous run to reach it. He is under that ball and waiting when it snaps into his glove.

The crowd cheers like I knew they would. They cheer because they would never have asked more of me than this. I have given them their heart's desire and I have done it on a day when I should not have had to. I am walking to the dugout with my head held down because I do not want the cameras to see the tears that are streaming down my face. I tip my cap and wipe my eyes on my sleeve and they scream for me. They scream. If someone had told my father when I was a boy that one day I would start a World Series game and that I would not fold and that I would pitch six innings and allow two runs and they would cheer for me like this, he would have been so happy. He would have been proud. My father would have been proud.

Bottom of the Sixth.

I do not care about anything going on in the game right now. I do not care how we hit. I do not care who is batting. I go find the end of the bench and I sit down and I cry. I do not sob. I do not make noise. I sniffle just a bit as the snot drips from my noise. I have tried to position myself so that cameras can't see me, but I know, somewhere, one is trained on me. I don't look for it because I don't want to know for sure. I hate knowing that there will be footage of my crying later. That sports shows will use this in a teaser to get more viewers. My father's death will be exploited for ratings. People will write commentary about it as though it is something about which commentary should be written. I think about this and it makes me angry enough that the tears start to dry and I start to see what is happening.

Brian is hitting. I want to see Brian hit. I know he would be sitting next to me if he didn't have to hit, but I want to see him hit. It doesn't matter that he's not as good as he once was. Not if you're just watching for pleasure. He still has the look. The grace in his swing. I notice there is a new pitcher. A tall, lean kid. Joel St. Onge. This is his first year, but he's done well. They wouldn't put him out there if they didn't think they had a real shot at winning. He throws harder than I do. I hope Brian can handle it. I watch him swing and miss at a fastball to start the at-bat. Another fastball misses, but Brian swings anyway, misses badly and is down in the count no balls and two strikes. He's starting his swing early to compensate. A little slower and he could still keep up, but these are coming in at ninety-eight, ninety-nine miles an hour. St. Onge touches a hundred often enough. Brian is smart, though. He knows after looking bad on two fastballs, he's going to see another one. He gets it out into left field for a nice little single. I'm glad he's on, even if I'd like to have him next to me right now.

I jump a little when I realize that Jerry is next to me. "How you doin', Zack."

"I'm fine, Jer."

"You looked a little shaky out there for a minute. Got any left in the tank?"

"I'll go as long as you need me." Of course I have some left in the tank. I have everything left in the tank.

"Don't be brave. You've had a great day. Your dad would be proud of you."

I narrow my eyes and stare at him and think, *who are you? Who are you to talk about what would make my dad proud?* "I'm fine," I say. "I can give you another inning, at least."

"All right, then. I can't ask more than that."

I'd pitch forever. I'd throw into extras. I'd never stop. I don't want to stop.

Carver is up and I haven't been paying attention. He hits a grounder to third. It looks like a double play, but the third baseman has to double pump and they only get Brian at second. He says a few words to Jerry that I can't hear and then he comes and sits next to me and I relax.

"Jerry says you've got another inning." As he says this he bends and starts putting his shin guards back on. Being a catcher means constant wardrobe changes.

"That's what I told him."

"You haven't thrown that many pitches today, but are you sure you've got more in you?"

"I could throw all night."

"Don't be a hero, Zack." He moves to the other shin guard.

"Who's being a hero? I just feel good. My stuff is still good."

"You know, what I said out there is true. You don't have to do any more than you've done."

"I know. I can do as much as I want now. I feel good."

"Okay. Good. Let's see how much you've got."

Brian is quiet and takes to watching the game, but he stays next to me. There's a friendliness to it. The way he sits relaxed beside me. There could be beers or maybe an open bottle of bourbon in front of us. Maybe I'll come out and stay with him for a while in the offseason. I did that last year. He has a wife and a couple of kids and a big place down in Florida. It's nice in the winter. Warm. You can run outside, and his kids are sweet. I've been afraid of kids for a long time, but I don't know. Maybe I could do it differently.

* * *

Dad and I had a good couple of years in high school when he was helping coach, but I should have known it wouldn't last. For those few years, our interests were in sync. The team was good, but not great, and we were never a real threat to go beyond regionals because I couldn't pitch every game, and we never had much offense. So those years, it was all about my development. Refining my control. Trying to add off-speed pitches. But senior year was different.

One of our other pitchers was a year behind me. Chad Bailey. He was solid against the lesser teams, but he didn't have much velocity so the more developed hitters could pound him. But he grew four or five inches in a year and suddenly added seven miles an hour to his fastball. No one saw it coming, but it gave us two pitchers who most other teams couldn't handle. The other, less surprising, thing was that our first baseman started hitting the ball a mile. We knew it would come eventually, he'd been slowly bulking up, but he finally hit a kind of critical mass. It was a perfect storm kind of year, and we all knew there was a chance we'd win state. It doesn't get much bigger than that in high school. Especially a small high school. As much as Indiana is all about basketball, our school forgot about basketball for a while. We were better than they had ever been.

We killed almost everyone in the regular season. We lost a few games when we had to use our number three pitcher and I remember I had a game where I couldn't hit the broad side of a barn, but otherwise, I don't remember anyone being able to touch us.

We were all giddy about it. When you're seventeen or eighteen and everyone in your school is paying attention to you—especially the girls—and there are even scouts showing up to watch you pitch, it feels like the world belongs to you. We were lucky that the playoff schedule was such that you needed only two pitchers. Each round was two games and the rounds were a week apart. We breezed through sectionals. That wasn't anything special for us, though. Regionals was the big hurdle. We'd never had the pitching we needed to make it through. I pitched the first game and it was great. I pitched a complete game. I needed only sixty or seventy pitches because I was on and those games are only seven innings. They got one run almost by accident and we won 6-1. Chad won the second game and we were on to semi-state. This is where the problems started. It rained during semi-state and the schedule got all screwed up. Chad pitched the first game, but it was four days before we could play the second. I was as rested as I could be, but I pitched only five innings because we were blowing them out and, as I would find out soon, the coach had plans he had not told my dad about.

*　*　*

Manny is up and even though we are winning, he is still swinging for the fences and is in the process of striking out in embarrassing fashion. Brian says, "Somebody needs to remind him he's not as big as it says he is in the media guide."

"He's hit a few."

"A very few. He's wasting at-bats."

Brian has this side. It's why he's still good enough to start. He is incapable of overestimating the abilities of anyone on his team, including himself. He always assumes he is slower than he is, that Russell doesn't have as much power as he does. Most of the other guys try to avoid talking to Brian about hitting because they don't want to hear him tell them what they're doing wrong. He wants to coach or manage later. I know this, though no one else does, but he needs to soften a little if it's going to work. People want to hear that they've done well sometimes.

He's just as hard on himself, though. He's lost a lot of bat speed now, but he had a good line this year because he can still out-think most pitchers.

"How bad did he have you fooled with those first two pitches?"

"The first time was just as bad as it looked."

He doesn't say anything else, but I see him smiling because he wants me to ask about the second time.

"Not the second time, though."

"My bat's not that slow."

"I'm glad you're on my side."

"Give it another year or two and you'll wish you could pitch to me. I won't be able to keep up with your weak shit."

"My what?"

"You heard me. You lost three-tenths off your fastball this year."

"You never turn off."

"Never."

* * *

We were having practice the day before the first game of state when everything went bad. We all assumed there'd been some discussion about how the pitching would be set up, but no one knew what the decision would be. I knew something was a little off when the coach walked up to me the moment my dad went off the bathroom.

"Big game tomorrow," he said.

"I know. I think we'll get through it, though."

"You've been with us for four years, Zack. I'd love to send you to the pros with your first real championship."

This had become a popular idea around the school and especially within the team. Scouts had been around all year, and I'd talked with some of them. The state tournament mattered because they wanted to see me against top-level competition. Dad, typically, had been circumspect about the draft. We'd enter, probably, but he wasn't sure about it.

I was seventeen and, of course, could not have been more enthusiastic about winning a state championship. "Yeah, coach. I'd love that."

"I think our best shot is going with Chad in the first game. Chad's been awfully good this year, but if we make it all the way to the end, I want you on mound."

I smiled broad and stupid.

"I know you'll be on short rest by a day."

"I don't care, Coach. I'll be fine. I'll bring it home."

Coach reached out and patted me on the shoulder. This is the kind of faith every athlete wants to inspire. I'd told him right there I'd do it. I didn't check with Dad. As far as I was concerned it was my decision.

* * *

Adam is up now with two outs and Carter shuffling around out at first base. Brian, apparently, has decided to offer a steady stream of commentary—maybe he's trying to relax me. "Poor kid. He only has a couple of good years left, and he doesn't even know it.

"Adam? He's only twenty-nine."

"Second basemen, man. They get old fast."

"Adam takes care of himself, though."

"It's not about that. He lives right on the edge. He doesn't hit homers. He's good at positioning, but he doesn't have a ton of range. It doesn't last forever."

I shake my head at him. "It's nice while it does last, though."

"It is. And hey, we don't have to worry. I've got my big contract. You'll get yours next year from somebody."

I don't say anything because I don't want to think about the possibility of someone else being my catcher next year. Russell and I are both free agents this year, and not many people think the team will sign both of us.

"Anyway, Adam's good now."

Brian nods but doesn't say anything. As if on cue, Adam hits a ball to right center. Coates has a little run, but he gets to it.

* * *

"No."

"What do you mean, no?"

But Dad isn't answering me. He's already off to tell his decision to Coach. I follow as soon as I come to my senses, but they are already raising their voices by the time I get there.

"We may never have another chance at this."

"I don't care about your small town ambitions. Zack is going places. I won't have you messing with his arm."

142

"It's one day. One start on short rest isn't going to end his career. And he already said yes. It ought to be his decision."

"Maybe it ought to, but he's still seventeen, and that makes it mine."

I'd heard enough at this point and decided to assert myself. "I want to pitch."

"That's nice to know, Zack, but I'm not going to let you."

"I'll be eighteen in two weeks."

"You're not eighteen now, son. And I'm glad. Do you really want to risk messing up your pro career for a stupid state championship?"

This did not sit well with me. Dad may have thought that all we had been doing for four years was working on my development, but I had also been trying to win every time out and I had really been trying to win in the playoffs. A state championship seemed a lot like the World Series to me at that point. I didn't care about my pro career. I cared about winning. I cared about doing what my coach asked. I wanted my dad to shut up. He was still standing there talking to Coach. He was calm as everything. I didn't hear what they were saying, but the longer Dad talked, the madder I got. Eventually, he turned to me. "Why are you still here?"

"I want to pitch!" I didn't shout at my dad. Not ever. But I shouted that.

He was unmoved. "Not happening."

I hated how calm he was. I wanted him to be mad. I shoved him so hard he fell over. "It's my choice!"

I hadn't seen Dad angry in a long, long time. Not like this. I was a tall, strong high school kid, but my dad had the strength you can only get from years of hard manual labor. He stood up and came toward me fast. He picked me up by my jersey and threw me ten feet. I landed on my ass and flipped. He walked up to me as I lay there and I was scared.

He stood over me. His fists were clenched. His arms and legs twitched as if he was only just able to restrain himself.

"You idiot. Don't you ever attack me. If you do that again, I'll beat you with a tire iron and then we'll see how your career goes. I said you're not pitching and you are not pitching. Get used to it." Then he turned and walked away. I lay there on the ground and watched him walk all the way to his truck, get in, and leave.

As I finally stood, I realized this mess had played out in front of the entire team. I had no idea what to do with myself. No one came up to me. Even Coach just stood there and stared at me. Wise or not, I decided the best way to defuse the tension was to go into the dugout and destroy everything I could get my hands on. Coach waited for me to finish, then he made me clean it all up. By the time I was done, everyone else was gone. He drove me home.

"As much as I don't like it, Zack, it is your dad's decision. We'll still go with Chad in the first game. We'll just have to cross our fingers about that second game."

I didn't respond so much as I made huffy sounds of discontent. Dad had never used force with me before. Never. He never would again, either, but that moment and what followed ruined things for us for two years.

When Coach dropped me at home, I was scared to go inside. I peeked in the garage first to make sure Mom was home, too, and even then I shuffled around on the porch for a minute before I went inside.

When I came in, Dad was sitting in the living room watching a taped game. He looked straight at me, completely unassuming, and said, "How'd your extra work go, Zack?"

Mom was there, too. She got up and gave me a hug. "I know you're disappointed that you won't get to pitch in state."

I think she expected me to say something, but I had no idea what was going on.

"It says a lot about what people think of you that your coach won't send you on short rest. Everyone thinks you're going places, Zack."

So there it was all laid out. Dad had beaten me home and told Mom a lie and there was no way for me to tell her otherwise. What was I supposed to say? "Hey Mom, what really happened is that

Dad wouldn't let me pitch, so I shoved him, and then he threw me halfway across the field and threatened to break my arm with a tire iron." Wouldn't fly. No point. His story made more sense than the truth. I clomped off to my room which, in her eyes, was a perfectly normal response to being told by my head coach that I couldn't pitch.

State went, well, you can fill in the blanks. Chad got us through the first game just fine, but our third best pitcher had no business pitching for a state championship. He got shelled badly and we lost 9-3. That wasn't even the worst part of it. There were scouts hanging around throughout the playoffs and before the game one of them asked me why I wasn't pitching.

"I would have been on short rest."

"That young arm can't go a day early when it needs to?"

I didn't know what to say. I didn't want him to think I was weak, but it felt weird to blame my dad. That didn't stop me from doing it, though.

"Your dad have a lot of influence on you?"

"I guess he's been coaching me since I was a kid."

I didn't understand at the time how important that conversation was. For months, Dad had been on me to go to college instead of the draft. He said the competition hadn't been good enough and all the reports we saw had me listed as a second-round pick at best.

"You go to college for a few years and then see how they like you. You'll go first round. Plenty of bonus money."

I told him I didn't care about bonus money and he told me not to be stupid. A team wasn't going to give up on me if it had a lot of money behind me. This was how the world worked and I'd better learn to see it.

Still, I'd put off committing anywhere while I waited to see where I was drafted. I didn't commit because I wanted teams to know that my first priority was going pro. On draft day we waited and waited for a call. I sat in the living room all day with my dad watching his DVDs of the '76 World Series. Well, he watched the DVDs. I watched for a while, and then I stared at him. When he bothered to look at me he would only smirk. I didn't go in the first round or the second. I fell all the way down to the sixth round. The Astros took me.

I don't know if Dad had planned it this way, but he knew about the conversation with the scout. He knew what I took a few years to figure out—that every major league team either thought I was soft or that I'd want my dad along as a coach wherever I went. Both of those were a lot to put up with for a high school pitcher who'd had almost no experience against top-flight competition, stuff or not.

It was hard to let Dad win. I talked to the Astros. They didn't offer much bonus money, but they said they thought I had a lot of potential. I could tell they weren't really that excited about me. I had "make-up issues." They expressed reservations about my occasional control problems—as though all hard-throwing high school pitchers don't have control problems.

Dad threw a college brochure down in front of me. "This is good program. Top ten for the last four years. You've got a scholarship there if you want it."

I didn't reply to him. I'd barely spoken to him since the incident on the field. I didn't need to tell him he'd won.

I went to college.

's are out. Time to work. Here we go. Look at m
u go. He can't touch   ow can he miss it?
n't believe he's not   It's time to work. A
can't touch it. Okay,   we go. Don't take the
ok at me, Dad.   w hard I can throw.
uch me. No s   A nice little jog. I h
e the seats I   me to work. Do you
d? There we   w walk. I can't believe
e. Listen to   an he miss it? Can y
Dad? Sparro   He can't touch it. It's
. Always go si   we go. I hope you like
got you. Look   d. Listen to them. Alwa
en is better. He   . Look how hard I can
see me, Dad? N   alk. Listen to them. Spa
ope. you like. th   got you. I can't believ

Top of the Seventh.

Slow everything down, just one more time, because this is the end. Start with the scrape of cleats on concrete steps. Next, feel the way the stadium opens up. The excited hum of the crowd knowing that the game is drawing to a close. Knowing that my start is drawing to a close. My hand slides into my glove as I step out onto the turf. My cleats sink in as I jog to the mound. Manny, running past me, remembers his self-selected role as my guardian angel. A slap on the butt. "I told you we would score for you. See, everything is okay. One more and then you rest." Step over the foul line. Take two steps to the top of the mound. Catch the ball

Brian throws out. Relax and begin my warm-up pitches.

* * *

For two years, Dad lost me. I was at college. I avoided his calls. My only goal was to play baseball. I didn't care about my education. I spent all my time at the athletic complex. I wanted to shake any idea of being soft or being under Dad's control. Whenever possible, I communicated with him through Mom or Kristen. Dad was having none of it. Whenever he could, he traveled to watch me play. When he couldn't, he called after the game. At the time, I preferred it when he came to games. Not because I liked seeing him—I would not have admitted to that—but because I didn't have to talk to him. I would hear him cheering from the stands, but at the end of the game, it was easy to walk past him. I might acknowledge him with a nod, but I didn't want to hear what he had to say about my performance. The phone was harder. I picked up, usually, because Mom called often enough and I had no problem with her. When it was Dad, he'd launch right into it. On the rare occasions he was able to get a game on TV, it was even worse, but he was always amplified. He'd go on and on about my pitch selection or mechanics, but he never paused to let me talk and he never asked me a question.

* * *

I am facing the bottom of the order. Leaving a
pitcher in for the bottom of the order is an easy
decision. Lynch steps in. This should be easy.
Bottom of the order. One more inning. Get into
the dugout. I am supposed to be pitching, but my
brain is somewhere else. Brian gestures out to me.
I shake it off and throw a fastball and get a strike.
He throws the ball back, and I'm slow again. I'm
looking for sparrows. I need to see a sparrow.

* * *

He never asked a question because he didn't want
to give me a chance to get off the phone. I don't
know what that meant. I don't know why he had
to talk about my pitching so badly. I had coaches.
Good coaches, too. We were a good program, but
they never overworked any of us. I knew to watch
out for that, but they were good. Dad would go on
and on anyway and when he was done, he'd hand
the phone straight off to Mom because she "wanted
to ask me some things." Mom and I would have
totally normal conversation about my classes and
how the game went and all that.

* * *

My next pitch is a slider and Lynch hits a
grounder to Manny for the first out. One down, two
to go, but I am still looking. In the rafters and the
stands. Everywhere. I want to see a sparrow or any
kind of bird. It's stupid. I know it is, but I can't
help myself. I keep looking around, trying to find

something. It's been a part of my life for so long. Even in college, when I wasn't talking to him and I was trying to ignore him talking to me from the stands, I could always pick out that word. Sparrow. Sometimes it was joyous. If I was pitching well and the other team could do nothing against me, he would shout, "The sparrows are really out tonight, Zack." If there were a couple of men on and the game was tight, he might tell me to look at the sparrows. "Time to work, kid. Time to work."

Togneri-Jones steps in and I can hardly keep my mind on the game or the pitch. The first pitch is a ball and the second one is a ball. Brian sees that something is wrong and he calls time and comes out.

"You okay out here?"

"I'm fine."

"You don't look fine."

"I'm fine. I just need to adjust. I'm not used to this."

"Not used to what? You've been out here for six innings already."

I want to know how he can suddenly be so thick-headed, but maybe he is trying to distract me. I repeat that I am fine, that I will calm down, and I send him back to the plate. I try to focus. I try not to think about what is missing. He is holding down one finger. Fastball. I start my windup. I try to feel all of it. The batter swings and misses. The ball comes back. One finger again. Fastball again.

Swing and miss again. The count is even. Easy. Easy like it should be. Then a foul. Then a foul. Then I miss a little and the count is full. With the next pitch, I walk him.

* * *

Near the end of my sophomore year, I threw a no-hitter. It was on the road and Dad wasn't there. When my phone rang, I knew who it was. I didn't want to hear him. I didn't want to talk about it. I didn't want to know if he thought I'd been great or just lucky. I wanted to celebrate with my team-mates and forget about Dad. He kept calling. I kept sending him to voicemail. He kept calling. Finally, I excused myself from the room and picked up.

"Hello."

"Hi, Zack. It's your Mom. I know you're out celebrating, but your dad and I wanted to tell you how proud we are of you. It wasn't on TV, but we listened to every pitch on the computer. Your dad didn't sit down for the last three innings."

"Oh. Thanks. Uh, thanks, Mom."

"Well, I won't keep you. Have fun tonight."

"Okay, Mom. I will."

"We love you, Zack."

"I love you, too... Um, Mom?"

"Yes, honey?"

No. I couldn't. "Never mind. Love you. Bye."

* * *

Jerry Newhall is up now, and I need to get him out. The lineup is about to turn over. Unless there's a double play, Ramirez will be up next. I don't want to think about that.

* * *

I got a call from Kristen the next day. "Hey little brother, you had yourself a game last night."

"I was okay."

"Dad must have talked your ear off."

"No. Um, I only talked to Mom."

"No way."

"Well, I missed the first call because we were out and I guess I didn't feel my phone vibrate. That might have been him. But it was Mom the second time."

"That's weird. Is he okay?"

"I think so. Mom didn't say anything. It was probably just late. You know Dad has to get up early."

* * *

I get behind again. Two balls and a strike. I shouldn't be working from behind like this, but I'm starting to lose it a little. I'm getting tired, I think. But I want to finish. Newhall helps me out by swinging at a bad slider. He hits a little bouncer right to first. Alex doesn't have a play at second, but he taps on first base to get the second out.

Ramirez steps in. Again with his bounce. "Sparrows are out. Time to work." That's what Dad would say. I look out into the stands, but I can't find him. I throw a fastball and he fouls it back. One more out, and I'll have it. Two more strikes.

Dad always taught me to finish innings. He didn't like the look of a pitcher giving the ball up and leaving with his head down. "That's a slow walk," he said. "Don't make the slow walk. Finish your job."

Sparrows are out. Time to work.

I can't believe he's not here. I threw a no-hitter last time and he's not here. He can't really be that mad can he? I was celebrating. I should get to celebrate sometimes. I shouldn't always have to check with him.

The next pitch I throw is a slider. Ramirez doesn't swing and the count evens up.

Where is he? Doesn't he know what kind of game this is? I should have picked up his call last time, but I just wanted to have fun. He never let me have fun. Remember the state championship, Dad? That would have been fun. Everyone would have cheered for me like they're cheering for me now. I wouldn't have broken. I've never gotten hurt. I've never been on the disabled list. I could have done it, it was a just a day early.

The next pitch is a ball, too, and I am behind in the count now.

Where is he?

Another ball.

Dammit! Where are the sparrows? I need to work. I need to work.

I walk him. Here comes Jerry out of the dugout. There's somebody getting warm out there. He's not moving too fast though. Good. They aren't taking me out. They aren't. He just wants to see that I'm okay. World Series. Late in the game. Lot of pitches. Gotta check on me. I'll finish it, though. No slow walk for me. I'll jog off when I get this last out. I'll jog off like you're supposed to. Here comes Brian too. We need to talk about strategy.

Everything is really clear again. It's like when the game started. The crowd is all rumbly and on edge, but that's okay. I can smell the food. It's cold, but the hotdogs and the popcorn make it feel not so cold. It would be nice to sit out there in the stands with Dad and be warm in a jacket with a hotdog. I bet they're selling hot chocolate, too. That's not really a baseball drink, but it would be nice. I can't believe he isn't here. Here's Jerry, though.

"How you feelin', Zack?"

"I'm okay. Missing my spots."

"You wearing out?"

"No. I feel good. I feel real good."

"What do you think, Brian."

"His stuff is still good. You're dropping your arm a little though, Zack. You're wearing out."

"No, I'm fine." See, there they are. Over on top of the dugout. A couple of little sparrows just like we used to have at the house.

"Anyway, we've got Coates coming up. I'm not worried about him, but listen, Zack, he's your last batter. I don't want you facing Ferris with the bases loaded."

"I'm not coming out before the inning's over."

"Get Coates and we won't have to worry about it."

"I'm not coming out, Dad."

"What?"

What did I say? "I said I'm not coming out, Jer."

"Just get Coates."

And then he looks at Brian and Brian nods at him and I think I hear one of them say something, but I don't know.

"Sparrows are out. Time to work. Let's work, Brian."

Brian taps me in the gut and says okay and jogs back to the plate just as the ump is about to break us up. And I settle in for Coates. I lookout over the dugout and the sparrows are just dancing. They look so happy. I bet they're getting lots of popcorn and sunflower seeds. I bet they're living high. Time to work. Brain calls for a slider and I like that because I don't want to mess around. Hell yes, a slider. Here you go. He waves at it. He can't touch me. He can't touch me. Time to work. Brian wants a fastball now and I throw it and it goes just a little high and the count gets all even. Boy, Dad is going to be sorry he missed this. I can't believe he's not here. The World Series, and right after I threw a no-hitter. How can he miss it? How can he miss it? It's okay, though. I know how to do it myself, Dad. I learned. It took a long time, but I learned. When it gets tight like this, I just look around and try to find a bird. Best if it's a sparrow, but any little songbird will do. I just find one of those and I know it's time to work. It's time to work right now. Brian calls for another fastball, and I let this one go. I mean, I really let it go. Coates can't touch it. He swings, but he can't touch it. Can. Not. Touch. It. I am bad right now. I'm humming. I bet Dad wishes he were here. I bet he's watching on TV. But that's okay. We'll talk tonight. After I win a World Series game. A World Series game, Dad, look at me. Almost through seven. You knew. You knew how important seven was. You told me to take some off if I needed to, so I could go deeper into games. People will complain about five or they'll praise you for seven. That's what you said, so I learned to control it better. Always go six. That's the job. Always go six. Seven is better. Don't take the slow walk. Brain wants a change-up, okay, here we go. Coates just catches it. Just a little foul. Almost had him. Almost. Almost. That's okay. I'm working. The sparrows are out. Look at them dancing on the dugout. Look at them. Dad can see them though. He's right there behind the dugout. Look at me Dad. Look at this. Look at what I'm about to do.

The World Series, Dad. And a no-hitter. Look, Dad. Look. Look how hard I can throw. They can't touch me. Brian wants a slider. Yeah. That's good. Let's finish him with a slider. Here you go. Here you go. Oh come on, now. The crowd doesn't like that one. That should have been a strike. Why are you calling it a ball. When I was a kid and we would listen to games on the radio, Dad would always chuckle because the umpires were sponsored by an eye doctor. Do you remember that Dad? What was the guy's name? The one who sponsored the umpires? What was his name? I'll ask after the game. When we're celebrating. We can have drinks now. Not like when I was a kid and it was milkshakes at the cheap place because money was always tight and what the hell difference did it make where the milkshakes came from. I'm going to buy you a new truck, Dad. And you won't need it because I'll pay people to work for you, but you'll have it. Look at this, Dad. Can you believe it? The World Series. Brian wants a fastball. I have to throw a fastball. This is it. Let's get it done. No slow walk. We want a nice little jog while they cheer. A nice little jog. Here you go. Hard as I can. There we go! There we go there we go there we go! I did it, Dad! I struck him out. Seven innings. In the World Series. The sparrows were dancing. Did you see them? Right in front of you? Look at me, Dad. I'm jogging off. No slow walk. No sir! I'm jogging. And they're cheering. Listen to them. Should I tip my cap? Damn right I should! Listen to them. They love it. They love me. Look what I did for them. Did you see it, Dad? I wish I could talk to you right now. We'll talk after the game. I hope you like the seats I got you. Oh I'm tired. They're cheering loud and everyone here in the dugout is high-fiving me and telling me I did a good job. I need to sit down. I need to close my eyes for just a minute. I feel shaky. That was a big game. Did you see me, Dad? I need to sit down. Did you see me?

Bottom of the Seventh.

Some of the luckiest moments are those in which we go unnoticed. I do not remember walking to the end of the bench. I do not remember sitting down, shoulder slumped against the wall. I remember sparrow chirps louder than any sparrow could be. Loud enough that it must have been inside my head. I remember seeing my dad in the stands surrounded by sparrows. I know I did not see this, but I remember it. No one else will remember it, but I remember it. I do not know precisely how long I spent with my eyes closed, unaware of what was happening around me, but it could not have been long. I open my eyes as the sparrow song fades and I see Takeda digging a throw out of the dirt at first. I have missed at least one batter. A moment later, Russell is announced and I know that it was only one. It was Matt I saw being thrown out at first. There is one out. There is a new pitcher on the mound, but I cannot see who it is. Things are fuzzy. I feel like I have finished a long night on the road. My eyes don't want to focus. I blink. I rub my palms across my closed eyes and pinch the bridge of my nose. I contemplate standing, but tingling in my legs advises me otherwise. I am not ready to refocus and I allow myself to fade back for another moment.

* * *

The draft happened not long after the no-hitter. I didn't hear from Dad between that game and the draft, but he knew. If we'd talked, we wouldn't have had any debates about it. The no-hitter happened against one of the best teams in the country. There were scouts in the stands. There could be no doubt. I was going to be drafted in the first round. Probably early in the first round. I had an agent ready to go as soon as it became official. He was the same one I'd talked to in high school. We'd stayed in touch, good foresight on his part, he was going to make a lot of money.

I knew everything was set, but it was still hard not hearing from Dad. It was the first time I missed him, maybe because it was the first time he let me miss him.

* * *

My head is clearing now and the real world is coming back into focus. I look out to the mound and I can clearly read the name on the back of the jersey. Franklin Ward is pitching. He pitched for us last year, but he got hurt and cut loose and like so many relievers found himself looking for a job in the spring. It's worked out well for him. He's pitching the seventh inning in a World Series. That is, he is a pitcher his manager feels confident in, and his agent gets to negotiate a new contract this winter. There are worse things.

He is also pitching to Russell.

* * *

As the season went on, the whole thing with Russell sort of faded into the background. I'll never believe how quietly it happened. There was never any guilt that could be proven. The case was dropped. There was a pennant race and Russell was having a good year, and so soon you started to have opinion pieces like this:

With his team pulling away from the pack largely because of his own MVP-caliber season, the question now becomes when Russell Jennings will sign an extension. Or, if things go bad, how they can expect to contend without him.

And then it would go on from there. It's unbelievable. I mean, look, some kid from the Dominican does steroids so he can be a major leaguer instead of a dirt poor kid from the Dominican and he's the devil, never mind that you'd probably never convict him of a thing. You can talk about how they aren't equivalent, I guess. How one isn't about the game. But it feels like a lie.

I can't talk. I never did anything. Kristen didn't let me forget it, either. Every time I talked to her, she'd mention Russell's season. "So it nice having the MVP on your team?" that kind of thing. Always with a bite in it that you couldn't miss. I don't like being that kind of disappointing.

* * *

But whether I like it or not, Russell is up and we might not be here without him. We won the division by four games. I guess we would have at least made the play-in game without Russell, but I don't see how we win the division without him. He's a great baseball player. He's showing how great he is right now, actually. Ward got a couple of strikes in on him early, but Russell has the count full now, and Ward has to decide if he's comfortable walking Russell. He is. The last pitch is a ball and it isn't even close. I can't say I blame him. I'd walk Russell right there, too. Don't want to give up another run.

* * *

Even around the clubhouse, people forgot. The guys who joked with Russell before joked with him again. The guys who always quietly respected his game, even if they thought he was kind of a jerk, still do.

I know just how Dad would have explained this to me given the opportunity. He would have used *Bull Durham*. Dad loved that movie. He hated the way Robbins couldn't pitch and he hated that they got some of the language wrong, but he loved the movie because he said it explained everything you needed to know about sports and baseball.

One game, during my first year in the minors, things weren't going well—I can't remember the exact situation, but they'd scored a few and there were still men on—I did my pace around behind the mound and melt down thing that I used to do and after the game Dad was quick to tell me I wasn't Nuke Laloosh.

"What are you talking about?"

"You haven't gotten called up to the show yet. You don't want them to think you're a head case. Be good first, then you can pace around behind the mound when someone gets on and they'll call you intense. You can destroy water coolers and yell at your teammates. You can do whatever you want once you're good. No one will care how you act."

"What about Barry Bonds?"

"They still cheer him at home."

He had a point. Dad was smart. No one cares what you do, if you're good. Or at least, the people who matter don't care.

That exchange is a good representation of what it was like to talk to Dad after I was drafted. In high school, he would have called me up and insulted me, but his tone was different now. He saw himself as more of an advisor. He never critiqued my pitch selection or my mechanics or anything like that unless I'd told them they were having me work on something. When they were having me work on something—especially my mechanics—I always told Dad because he'd seen me throw more than anyone. Once my coaches realized that Dad could be helpful, they'd tell me to tell him. They didn't want him in the clubhouse, but if he would spot the flaw in my delivery, well that was fine with them.

I was in the minors for not quite two years, and it was the first time in my life I felt like Dad and I had a good relationship. I wasn't afraid to talk to him about things. I was a baseball player. It was apparent to everyone involved that I would very soon be a major league baseball player. I didn't understand what had changed in Dad—I wouldn't understand it until it was almost too late—but I liked it.

* * *

Alex is up now and Brian is over next to me waiting to see if he should take off his gear and get ready to hit.

"Who's pitching next? Micah?"

"Yeah. Only two innings left. Might as well throw our best for an inning each."

I rock my head in affirmation.

"Are you okay? I had a feeling you weren't all together out there."

"I'm fine now."

Brian doesn't like this answer. It tells him he was right when he wanted to be wrong.

"Did you call Jerry 'Dad'?"

"I might have, yes."

"He should have taken you out." Why he says this to me when professing concern about my mental state, I don't know.

"I got through the inning."

"You did. You did. Hell of a thing."

"Gotta be tough, right?"

This is a joke between us. Brian says I complain about hangnails like I need Tommy John surgery. "You wouldn't know tough if it fell on you."

"You've gained too much weight. I wouldn't want to risk injury."

We laugh together. Alex works the count in front of us. We go quiet in that way you do when you know you've allowed yourself to forget something. We watch Alex at the plate. The count is full when he lifts a fly ball to left. It is an easy out.

* * *

Brian had an interesting reaction to the Russell situation. It was a lot like Dad's, but there was more honesty in it. I asked him if he thought I should say something to the press.

"You told the investigator guy what you heard, right?"

"I wasn't the only one who heard it."

"I know, I know. I heard it too, and I told the guy. And what did he do about it?"

I didn't say anything to this.

"Exactly. Dude did it. He raped the girl. The DA's office knows it, but can't convict or doesn't care to try. What's talking to the press going to do?"

"Might make it easier for the girl?"

"Bullshit. Her life is not going to be affected by anything you do. Guy's a rapist. He's going to keep playing ball. If he goes near a woman I know, I'll beat him with a bat."

Okay, I guess Dad didn't threaten to beat Russell.

"Don't you feel bad, though? We win games because of him?"

"So? I can't control who I work with. I love baseball, but it's a job. Jerks are everywhere."

This is Brian. Sometimes he makes me uncomfortable.

* * *

Hector is up now. Brian is technically in the hole, but he is reclined next to me, his shin guards untouched. We continue our silence, but the tension has drained out of it. We are watching a baseball game. We are leading. It's late in the game and, at the moment, it has the feel of a game that's already won. Our bullpen is great. It's not a huge lead, but we don't give the lead up a lot. So, it's as relaxed as it can be up four to two in a World Series game. Something will happen to change that. A runner will get on or the crowd will get excited. But right now, it is calm.

* * *

Russell and I, strangely enough, debuted on the same day. We were both late season call-ups. I had been talked about for a while, of course, but Russell had outperformed his expectations. He was drafted out of high school in the second round, so it's not like they expected him to be chopped liver, but he got here fast. The minor leagues just couldn't hold him.

Russell or no Russell, the day I debuted, everything in my life got better. The thing about being a baseball player is that you have no idea how it's going to work out. Can't-miss prospects miss all the time. Injuries happen or a guy just can't make the leap. If you're a pitcher, a little twinge in your shoulder happens and it's over before you get started. And then what? You're young, sure, but you probably haven't studied real hard and you have to start all over. That's always a possibility until it happens. And that day it happens, well that's a big day.

There's nothing interesting to say about my debut. I was a little nervous, but not terribly so. I pitched okay, though I made it only five innings. The team was bad and had put me in the rotation to see if I would be ready to help next year, but my innings were being watched. I wouldn't be allowed to throw too much. What was important and different about that day was how it affected things with my family.

Dad, obviously, was thrilled. But things had been kind of weird with Mom and Kristen for a long time. Mom did the typical mom thing where she worried about my career. She didn't like how little the minors paid—never mind the huge signing bonus I'd gotten—and she worried about me never making it, about me getting hurt. Washing out at twenty-five without even a cup of coffee. Seeing me on the mound in a major league game meant she could relax a little more. People talk about the league minimum like it's not that much, but in the month I was up, I made more than either of my parents ever made in a year. That made Mom happy.

Kristen was different. Things with her were always complicated. Like I said, she should have been the baseball player in the family. She has a Pete Rose kind of mind. She's totally driven. But as a girl, there was just no way it was going to happen.

No one would even look at her for college. She tried to latch on with a semi-pro team, but I think Mom guilt-tripped that out of her. One kid trying to make it as a baseball player was hard enough. This was Kristen's life, pushing her dreams to the side so I could have mine.

Kristen has always been about the payoff, though, and the day I debuted, it meant all the sacrifice had been worth it.

* * *

Sometimes, when I'm out of a game, I lose track of what's going on out on the field. Mostly I pay attention, but I think a lot and sometimes I forget to watch. I have forgotten to watch Hector, but I am awakened from my thoughts by the general upheaval of our team taking the field. Hector stands near the batter's box waiting for his glove to be delivered. He has, it seems, struck out.

The transition between innings is something that never, ever changes. It is exactly the same now as it was in little league. Your team makes the last out. Everyone grabs their gloves, finishes their Gatorade, and trots out. Balls are tossed around and dropped and someone has to run after them. Generally, the execution is more precise than you see when you're a kid, but it has that same air. Just a little catch to get warm. To wake your brain from the torpor that comes from sitting on the bench. I would like to go back out, but it isn't going to happen. I have been relieved.

Top of the Eighth.

Our new pitcher is one Micah Lapping-Carr. Micah got a trial a few years ago as a starter, but he had only two pitches and that wasn't enough, so he was sent to the bullpen. He is now our man in the eighth inning of close games. One day, perhaps soon, he will graduate and become a closer. Like so many relievers today, he throws hard. This is the only weapon anyone believes in right now. Speed. Power. I can't complain, since I make my living off that very thing, but it is nice to see the few guys out there who get by with less. Who are very good without throwing very hard. Micah throws hard, but what really makes him good is his change-up. It is routinely a full fifteen miles per hour slower than his fastball and batters can never tell the difference. His arm action is exactly the same. And so, they guess. If they are wrong, they look foolish. If they are right, his stuff is still hard to hit. I would rather be in the game, but I am glad to have him out there when I'm not.

* * *

When I first came up, Dad's only remaining fear was that I would become a relief pitcher. He said pitching in relief was too much about what you can't do and that teams didn't know how to handle them. "Look how fast they flame out," he said. And I'd point out Mariano Rivera and he'd point out, justly, that there weren't many like him around. He also liked to point out that decent fourth starters routinely get more money than free agent relievers.

But it wasn't much of a fear. I was close to a finished product when I was drafted. I still had occasional control issues, especially with my slider, but I had three pitches and they were all good pitches. There was very little chance of me being sent to the bullpen. Too much was invested in me.

I have been a lucky exception in that my career has gone the way it was supposed to. This was true right from the start. I started five games during my cup of coffee. I was generally pulled after five, but once I was allowed to go seven because my pitch count was so low. I struck a lot of guys out and walked a few more than the team would have liked, but there was nothing about me that was going to keep me out of the rotation. Whatever further development was going to happen would happen in the majors.

Regardless of how finished I was, I've always envied the role of the ace reliever. There's something cool about it, in a way that cannot help appealing to the juvenile part of my brain. They get to pick their entrance music, and it gets played for more than the ten or fifteen seconds batters get. They get called in to pitch to the best hitters on the team because it is understood that even the best struggle against them. Micah is out on the mound to start the inning, but he was ready last inning. If Coates had gotten on, it was Micah, not me who would have faced Ferris, who steps in now looking as though he does not think this game is over. Looking like someone who knows how to keep a game like this going. Micah appears unfazed.

My envy for Micah is tied up a lot in Dad's view that no inning should go unfinished. I wish that no game had to go unfinished. I have six years in the majors and I have stood on the mound at the end of a game only five times. Only four of those were for a win. So much has been written about how good I am and how much I have helped this team win and yet, at the moment of victory, I am almost always on the bench watching.

I am watching now and Micah strikes Ferris out. Ferris works a full count first, but a strikeout is a strikeout. Relievers don't have to worry about pitch counts. It's fun to imagine what I could do if I only had to pitch one inning.

But I never have. I have never, if you can believe it, pitched in relief. Not in little league, not in high school, or college, or the minors. Never. Of course, I threw complete games all the time before I was drafted. That was easy; the hitters were usually so overmatched that if I didn't shoot myself in the foot, there was no reason to take me out.

But that first year or so in the major leagues, Dad was worried. It was a kind of sheepish worry and he didn't talk about it much, but he'd seen so many pitchers shifted to the bullpen that he convinced himself it might happen with me. Especially as I struggled to get my head under control.

There was one stretch during my first year when I had three bad games in a row. In two of them I didn't make it out of the third. It's the kind of thing that happens to every pitcher at some point, but it was my first year, so there were stories about how I still needed to develop my control or about my makeup or whatever.

Mom and Kristen weren't worried though. They were happy just to have me in the majors. That had always been the goal. Kristen was pretty thrilled because she'd started working with this thing called Baseball for All that gives girls opportunities to play baseball instead of softball, which is pretty cool. Anyway, as soon as I was called up, she was on me to come to events and camps and all that. I couldn't tell her no. She spent too many years holding a bat while I pitched. I've probably hit Kristen with more baseballs than everyone else I've ever faced put together.

* * *

Now that Ferris is taken care of, Micah is facing Marcus Martin. It's lonely on the bench, after a start. It's just me, the coaches, and the other bench guys, so I'm sitting by myself here watching a game.

One of the weirdest things about being a pro was that I almost never watched games on TV, and I never, ever watched them with Dad. When would I? Sometimes, on the road, if I was tired and didn't feel like going out, I'd turn on a late game and treat it as background noise. It was weird getting used to watching games on my own. Dad talked all the way through games, but watching by myself, it was easy to stay quiet.

There was a lot of quiet in those first few years. Sometimes, there would be a girl who I'd see for a while, but nothing that got serious. I've never been really good at talking to other people. I've always been more of a listener. Growing up with Dad, I didn't have much of a choice. You had to listen when Dad was around. But in the majors, he wasn't on me all the time. We talked, but it wasn't constant like it had been. From the way I lost it on the mound sometimes, I got the reputation of being kind of touchy, so no one really wanted to go out with me after games. I'm not complaining. I'm not a bar guy. I don't like clubs. It wasn't that I wanted to go out with the other guys on the team or whatever, it was that I didn't feel a part of things in the same way I thought they must.

Micah is a little bit like I was, I think. I try to talk to him about it sometimes, but it's hard when neither of you is really a talker. I think we might work out together a little during the offseason, though. And now he's struck out Martin, too. He's having a good night.

* * *

Thinking about it now, I wonder if the time after I went pro was as good for Dad and me as I thought it was. I mean, we didn't have any fights or anything and he was a lot calmer than he had been when I was a kid, but I was pretty lonely. I remember during a road trip my first year in the minors, we'd been on the bus forever—which is the story everyone tells, though it's plenty true—and I felt so incredibly lonely. Dad called and started talking about my start the next day and I wasn't up for it.

"It's lonely out here, Dad." This wasn't enough for Dad. I don't know why I even bothered, but I didn't feel like there was anyone else.

"What do you mean it's lonely out there? Sure it's lonely. You've gotta pay your dues, though."

This felt like the canned comments Dad was always on me to use in interviews, and I realize now that he didn't know what to say. Dad has never been lonely a day in his life. Dad finds people to talk to. I don't work that way. I take ages to get to know people and in the minors your teammates change all the time. They can shut you out, too. Especially when you move through the system like I did. Everyone's afraid you'll take his spot. With Dad, we'd talked about baseball because it was all we were concerned with, but somewhere along the line, it killed everything else, and once I was drafted, we found we couldn't talk about anything else. That's pretty rough.

I couldn't even joke with Dad. When I got my signing bonus, I did what every first-round pick does and bought a ridiculous car. What was I supposed to do? I was twenty. During my first full year in the majors, all this money was coming in and I have didn't know what to do with it. I mean, I know it's chump change compared to what I make now, but the first time you make half a million dollars, you are constantly aware that this is a great deal of money. At least you are if you come from a place like where I came from. I told Mom I wanted to pay off the house, but she wouldn't let me, "Save it, Zack. Save it." So I bought another stupid car and a nice condo, but there was still a lot of money. Dad asked what I was doing once and I told him I was sitting on the piles of money I didn't know how to spend. He didn't like that at all and got all indignant about how I should be grateful for all I had, especially after how hard he and my mother had worked and all that kind of talk. It was terrible. I didn't mean it like that. I just didn't know what to do with it. I really didn't. I still don't. Things like that stress me out. I do better when I know what is expected of me.

* * *

Apolinar is up now. If Micah gets him out, he will go home tonight having faced only Ferris, Martin and Apolinar. That's a night for you.

* * *

I was lucky I had Kristen. I am lucky I have Kristen, still. I was promoted to Double-A toward the end of my first year in the minors and Kristen called to congratulate me. We'd talked over the course of the year, but it hadn't been anything deep. Just keeping in touch.

"Hey, little brother, you're almost to the big leagues now."

"I guess."

"Whoa, now. Don't get too excited."

"I wish they'd waited until next year."

"Isn't it a reward, though. Isn't that why they promote players with a month to go?"

"Yeah, it's supposed to be. I'd rather finish where I am, though. I'm starting to get to know some of the guys here."

"So? Get to know some guys in Double-A."

"You know I don't work that way."

She stopped talking for a minute. Kristen and I didn't really talk about feelings. I don't really talk about feelings. I try not to have feelings. They are inconvenient.

"Are you okay, Zack?"

I'll spare the messy details of the conversation. They don't really matter. It was heartfelt. I talked about my loneliness. She told me to try to relax. I told her I didn't really know how to do that. She acknowledged the truth of what I said. It wasn't earth-shattering, but she started calling me every week after that. She didn't make a big show of it as charity. She talked to me about what was going on in her life. How she was trying to decide if she wanted to move. She asked me what I thought about different things in her life. That was my favorite part. No one ever asked me what I thought. I was always expected to follow directions. She listened sometimes, too, which was nice.

During the offseason we hung out a lot. She even worked out with me. This is what Kristen is like. She decides to do something and then she does it. Because I was lonely, she decided to be close to me and then she was. I never doubted it. There was nothing disingenuous about it. She doesn't do things she doesn't want to do. If she didn't like me, she wouldn't have done it. Kristen is different than Dad like that. With Dad, you always wondered how much was about you and how much was about him.

* * *

Micah gets Apolinar on a fly out. Why does he get such an easy inning off those guys? It doesn't matter. I did my job. I spent all night freezing out there on the mound, and I now I get to sit here with my jacket on, and there are heaters so even though it's a cold night, it isn't that cold. It doesn't matter if I'm cold right now, though. I can sit here all night and my muscles can get tight and chilly and it doesn't matter. I like being cold. I like being cold and not doing anything in it. Once I went pro and was completely out of Dad's hands, I stopped working out in the cold. That winter when Kristen and I worked out together, we were always in a heated gym. I'm happy to run on a track. Just because the sparrows are out doesn't mean I have to be out with them. I do my work. I always do my work. Kristen can tell you, we still work out together. My second summer in the minors, she called me and told me she missed me. Hard to believe. She asked how long I thought it would be until I got called up and even though I said I didn't know, she moved here. That is a crazy thing to do, but she said she needed to move to a city for work anyway, and she might as well be close to her brother. Kristen doesn't come to all of my games, but she comes to a lot of them. In some ways, it's weirder not to have her here tonight than Dad. He always had to travel. He mostly watched me on TV. After I got called up, it was really Kristen who took care of me.

I wish she'd been here tonight to take care of me, but I know she's watching at home. I know she'll call me when the game is over. Anyway, I don't need taking care of right now. Right now, my job is to sit here in my jacket near a heater and stay warm and watch my team finish off this game.

Bottom of the Eighth.

This should be our last time batting. Ward is out for a second inning. Not because they are giving up, but because he did not pitch last night and we have the day off tomorrow and he got through the middle of the order just fine last inning. He's good. He still has gas in the tank. He isn't going anywhere.

Dave is up first. Dave is the best kind of player to have up in this situation. He's been around a long time. He never gets too comfortable, nor does he relax entirely. He just is. He goes into every at-bat that same way, knowing what he can and cannot do against a pitcher.

I can imagine Kristen being like Dave when she gets a little older. They both have a steadfastness to them, though Kristen veers more toward stubborn than Dave. I'll never be like either of them. I fold easily. I wonder, sometimes, what kind of pitcher I'll be when I start to lose my stuff. I've never been good at accepting my limitations.

* * *

Kristen had a complex relationship with Dad. She resented a lot of things about him. His casual misogyny. How he lavished attention on my development while mostly ignoring her even though she worked harder than I did. These were not likable parts of Dad. But they are the same in a lot of ways, and that's what kept them close, I think. Dad wanted to be a baseball player, but he couldn't be, so he made me into one. Kirsten wanted to be a baseball player, but she couldn't be, so now she puts all her extra time into this nonprofit getting girls to play baseball. Those two things aren't so different. It's adjustment. Finding a different way to satisfy desire.

Kristen could see what other people wanted, though. I guess that's because she's a girl. I don't know if the world will let you be a girl and pay attention only to what you want. Dad wanted me to be a major leaguer. Kristen wanted herself to be one, but she also wanted Dad to have what he wanted, so she helped. What Kristen wanted never entered Dad's mind. I don't know if what I wanted did either.

For a long time, it was Dad who got the benefit of Kristen, but for the last few years, I have.

Everyone was there for my debut, of course, but after that, Mom and Dad went back home and it was only Kristen. I liked having her around during my first full year. The team was pretty bad and there were a lot of guys who knew this was going to be their last or their only major league job and I think the pessimism overwhelmed the clubhouse. There were plenty of days when I didn't like going to work, but Kristen was quick to remind me that it could be a lot worse and that teams can change in a hurry. It really takes only a couple of decent guys to make work fun again. So I held on.

Everyone knows that teams have a little section set aside for the families of players. Mostly, this is wives and girlfriends, but at the beginning, Kristen was there every time I pitched. Later, Sydney took over, but that's also mostly to do with Kristen, too.

* * *

Dave grounds out. No big deal. But Brian is up now and I want to pay attention.

* * *

If Kristen was the first part of what I needed to be successful, Brian was the second. I think all the time about how much he helped me on the field, but even though he's only six years older than me, he supplemented Dad really well.

Things with Dad were weird for a long time after I made it up. When I think about that part of my life, I don't think about Dad much at all. We talked about my games, but that was all. He started to come back into the picture the same year we signed Brian. It was the year I got my first big arbitration raise—we didn't go to arbitration, the team settled at the last minute—which was enough money that Mom couldn't tell me to put it all away. Both of my parents refused to quit working or to let me buy them anything new, but they did let me pay off the house for them. I think the gesture really moved Dad, but I didn't understand why. Brian had to explain it to me.

"It's because he knows you appreciate what he did."

"I've been trying to do this for three years. They just wouldn't let me."

"Did you think your parents would accept when you offered the first time?"

"No. I knew they wouldn't."

"Exactly. You re-offered when they didn't have a reason to say no. That matters."

"That's insane."

Brian reached over and tousled my hair like I was a kid. "You'll figure it out someday, Junior." He still drives me nuts with that crap, but he stopped calling me Junior when I won the Cy Young last year. He still puts himself in charge of me, though, which is ridiculous. I am a grown man or something close to it. I don't need him to tell me what to do. Except sometimes when I'm pitching. Or when I'm figuring out what to do with my girlfriend.

Okay, maybe he should be in charge of me.

* * *

He's fighting like crazy up there against Ward. A bunch of foul balls, but it's still only 2-2. He has to start his swing too early to work the count, but he keeps fouling bad balls off. This is something he's been working on. He wants to be able to make contact with balls out of the zone so he can when he has to. I don't know if it will work. He's not Vladimir Guerrero. This is what I tell him, but he shrugs and tells me I'll figure it out someday.

It's not going to work. If he was here next to me, he'd see what Ward's doing, working it farther and farther away from the strike zone until Brian swings at one he can't touch. But Brian's lost his head up there. He's too busy hoping for the good pitch instead of watching for the bad ones.

And finally, it happens, a fastball way out of the zone Brian looks bad swinging at it and flings his helmet down as he comes into the dugout. He sits down next to me and starts putting his gear on. "I don't want to hear about it."

"You know we're winning, right."

"Winning and having won are not the same."

"Always the pessimist."

"Talk to me when you're thirty-four." He's pulling the straps on his shin guards like they've done something to personally offend him.

"Is that when I'll start letting hitters work me like he worked you?"

He picks up his mask like he's going to hit me with it and for a moment I'm actually worried, but he sees me and stops. He smiles. "You asshole."

"You did exactly what he wanted you to do."

"Well hitters don't get to stop in the middle of at-bats and talk to coaches, do we?"

* * *

Brian does not admit defeat so much as he stops talking about how right he is. This is not the only way Brian is the same as Dad. Having Dad come back into my life willing to talk about things other than baseball was comforting, but combining him with Brian was strange. They both liked telling me what to do and they almost always agreed. They agreed on my pitching. They agreed about what kind of house I should buy. They agreed on how I should spend the offseason. The only thing they didn't agree on was girls.

I was never a guy who had half a dozen women—that's just not who I am—but I could get bored easily. There are a lot of great women out there, but the kind of women you meet when you're a ballplayer who is not really good at seeking out other people are the kind of women who are only interested in you because you're a ballplayer. These are not the most interesting people in the world. Brian always insisted I should try to find someone to keep around for a while. "You don't have to marry her. You can take your time, but a little stability helps, man. These guys you see trading women all the time, they get tired. I did that for a while. I got tired. Settle down. Have a quiet life. You're suited to a quiet life anyway."

Dad was, I think, permanently scarred by my middle school relationship with Ashley. Parents do this. At least my parents do. They grab onto certain moments in your life—things that happen long before you're finished figuring out what you're like—and they decide that this is How You Are. Dad did that with Ashley. He assumed that I was obsessive. That I could focus on only one thing at a time. To be fair, there was more evidence than just Ashley for this, but still, he didn't have act so terrified when I mentioned that I might want to try to settle down.

"I don't know, son. Lots of guys, they get a serious girl and they get all that money and they get distracted. Their game suffers."

Kristen would hear this and immediately point out all the different ways Dad was full of it, but I'm not Kristen, so I just got off the phone.

Dad would have preferred it if I'd just been celibate, but though he might have been unreasonable, he wasn't naïve.

As much as Dad and Brian were trying to push me in different directions with girls, it was Kristen who forced my hand during the All-Star break that year. Brian had offered to have me out to stay with his family during the All-Star break—that's a big gesture, guys don't get much time with their families during the season—but I declined because I had Kristen in town already and she'd told me we had plans since I didn't make the team—which was ridiculous, I was having a great year. That's not the point though. The point was that this was when I met Sydney. Sydney spent a lot of time in the stands for me. Sydney spent most of two seasons in the stands and I have not thought about her once tonight. I don't know what that says, but I don't think it's very good.

* * *

I don't get the chance to dwell yet, though. Brian taps me on the leg and says, "See you in a few," just as Coates grabs a fly ball from Carver's bat. We need to get only three more outs. I watch the bench empty and my team trot out onto the field.

Top of the Ninth.

Ramon Santiago is out to pitch. At times this year, our bullpen has been an issue, but we have always had two guys we could rely on. If you could get through seven with the lead, Micah and Ramon would take care of it almost every time.

Ramon is out to face the bottom of the order. The script should write itself. Premium closer. Bottom of the order. Two-run lead. This is not a game in much doubt. But still it is the World Series and even though we are objectively better than the other team, bad teams do not find themselves in the World Series. Caution is always merited. I used the laid back atmosphere of the eighth to recover but now, as I knew it would, the tension has returned. The crowd cheered loudly as Ramon trotted in from the bullpen and they have not stopped. Those of us still on the bench are sitting, but we are not reclined. Our backs are straight or we lean forward. Both cleats in contact with the ground.

Sydney had a fight with Dad about this kind of thing when they first met. We had been dating for four months when I brought her home for Thanksgiving. It was a big thing. I had never brought someone over for a major holiday. She wasn't really a baseball fan. Or she hadn't been. Kristen had convinced me to meet her by telling me, "Sydney doesn't even follow baseball. She doesn't even know who you are. I just told her my brother was nice. It's not even a set-up."

"It feels like a set-up."

"It's not a set-up. She's a good friend and I think you two would get along. You need friends, Zack. So does she. Neither of you gets out enough. And she's cute. Is that so terrible?"

"It's a set-up."

Kristen shrugged her shoulders. She didn't lie well.

It was true. Sydney didn't know who I was. She did tell me I seemed familiar and asked if we'd met before. When she asked why people kept staring at me, I feigned ignorance.

Sydney and I started seeing each other, as Kristen intended. And she, of course, learned why I seemed so familiar.

"I can't believe I let Kristen set me up with an athlete!" was the typical exclamation once we'd gotten used to each other. Sydney was the first person other than my mom who had nothing invested in how I did on the field. She wanted me to do well because that made me happy, but that's all it was about. She was much more interested in my long-dormant nerdy side, which she discovered in conversation with Kristen.

Like all good significant others, she learned about what I did and I tried to learn exactly what she did, though I believed her when she said it was "boring corporate security stuff," because, well, doesn't that sound boring? I gathered that she spent most of her time trying to prevent employees from downloading viruses and then cleaning up the mess when they inevitably did. My job was easier to engage with. The argument she had with Dad was the product of this relatively late-in-life engagement with baseball. She was a grownup and not inclined to accept standard doctrine.

"I don't understand why the crowd just erupts for someone who's coming in to get three easy outs at the end of the game."

"Oh, they cheer for everybody."

"But shouldn't they cheer the most for the player who has the hardest job."

"You just don't understand baseball."

Dad turned away after he said this but a little smile crept onto his face. He and Sydney had this same argument a lot. She'd gotten interested in all the advanced stats. She didn't like ERA. She thought the closer was stupid. Dad wasn't a dinosaur, but he didn't buy into all of that either. I could tell he liked having someone to argue about baseball with. Kristen and I had gotten tired of it ages ago and Mom never had the energy, but Sydney didn't back down from any argument and she read all the time. Dad used to tease her about that. "You're always telling me how you read something. You ever watch the game? Do that and you'll know why they cheer for the guy who gets the last three outs."

* * *

Ramon has gotten a lot of cheers this year and he gets the first out when Takeda strikes out looking. Now he just has to deal with Lynch and Togneri-Jones. The crowd is getting louder and louder. They won't quiet down until he gets the last out and the game is over.

Lynch steps in and takes his stance. Santiago throws a fastball and Lynch is way behind. He catches just a piece of it and sends it foul, but the next pitch, he starts his swing a little earlier. He's still behind but he's able to send it down the right field line. It's not a hard hit, but it's a solid one. He has deviated from the script.

The crowd only becomes more raucous. They aren't concerned. The eighth and ninth batters are coming up. They can still smell the win.

But that doesn't last long. Togneri-Jones steps in and does just what Lynch did but to the other side. A sharp little grounder into left and now there are two men on and the crowd is quiet. It is quiet because the minds of baseball fans are always several moves ahead. It goes like this: There is only one out. Unless Newhall hits into a double play, the lineup will turn over. That means you've got Ramirez, at least. It's not hard to imagine Ferris up, one run, possibly more, already be in. They will have a chance to turn the game on its head. This is baseball. It does not always go how it is supposed to go. I think there's a Twitter hashtag about that.

* * *

Sydney dove into all the online stuff. I try to stay away from it because so much of it is so stupid. You have one bad game and all of a sudden everyone is questioning your manhood and calling for you to be traded. It's a weird place. I mean, do these guys never have a bad day at work? But Sydney thought it was interesting. She kept telling me I just needed to learn how to filter what I saw. She wanted me to learn about the "data." I told her I knew about that stuff. We've all been on FanGraphs and Baseball-Reference and all those sites. It's not like we have our heads in the sand, but so much of it feels totally divorced from playing the game. At least it does to me. I mean, if I were a GM, I'd be all over this stuff, but as a player, I don't know how much good it can do me. Those sites all love me anyway, so I figure I'm already doing what I'm supposed to do.

Dad never got into computers at all. My parents had one, but Dad used it only to watch my games. That was the extent of his internet sphere. I wish I was as good at holding back on it as he was. But I can't just not get online. That would be weird.

Dad disagreed with pretty much everything Sydney said about baseball, but I think he liked her. He never pushed me to marry her or anything, but he also never talked about how I shouldn't divide my focus or any of the other crap he was always so quick to come out with. He respected that she was smart. Mom is smart and Dad always talked about how stupid it was for men to be afraid of smart women. Maybe that's what he was afraid of. Maybe he just wanted me to end up with some-one like my mom. Sydney's like Mom in some ways. I don't know.

* * *

Newhall does not ground into a double play. He does scare the entire stadium into total silence with a very deep fly ball that takes Hector all the way back against the wall at a run. He catches it, but he bashes into the wall awkwardly and both runners are able to tag up and advance.

Ramon doesn't speak English great and I don't speak Spanish at all so we don't talk much. I'd like to ask him about this moment though. About how he feels. I'd be freaking out and trying hard not to look like I was freaking out. But Ramon comes into situations like this all the time. He's supposed to love it. He's supposed to thrive on the pressure. Does he? Does he really love it or is he just trying to execute and relying hard on his stuff. That's what I do in those situations. And he doesn't have to worry about how many pitches he's throwing. He's here for just an inning. That can be fun. I got to start the All-Star game this year, and I knew ahead of time I was going to pitch only one inning, so I just let go. I got up over a hundred on a couple of pitches. It was great. I wonder if that's what it's like for him. Just fun. No need to think too much. Just throw and rely on your stuff.

But he's got to be thinking now, doesn't he? Ramirez is up and there are runners on second and third. There are two outs. It is the ninth inning. The crowd is scream, screaming, screaming. Ruh-Mone. Ruh-Mone. Ruh-Mone. He gets a chant. Closers get all the cool stuff even if they don't make as much money as starters do.

Ramirez is up and he can do serious damage. The only good thing is that he is not my problem. I am able to watch with a little less emotion his piston bounce and the perfect stillness as the pitch leaves the hand. His Rickey Henderson crouch that shrinks the strike zone to the size of a large apple. He works the count. Piston bounce. Stillness. Ball one. Piston bounce. Stillness. Foul. Piston bounce. Stillness. Ball. Piston Bounce. Stillness. Strike. With every strike the crowd gets louder. With two strikes, they are roaring. Two strikes and two outs and a great player up and the game on the line. This is the little boy moment, isn't? This is what we all wanted. The only difference was which side of the ball you were on. Brian was hitting against Randy Johnson. I was striking out Barry Bonds. I wonder what Ramon was doing? It doesn't matter now. He will always be facing Juan Ramirez. He stretches. It's a fastball. Everyone knows this. It's too far inside. The count is full. Everything feels pulled. Stretched. Ages and ages pass between pitches. The game is about to be over if only one more strike will come or a fly ball or a ground ball or a liner that Manny dives for and snags. It doesn't matter. Just an out. Any out will do. Ramirez bounces. Ramon stretches. Ramirez stills. Fastball. Everyone knows it. Ramirez knows it. His swing is fast. Everything about him is fast. He shoots a line drive over Adam. It takes one bounce between Matt and Russell before it hits the wall. The game is tied. There is no question about that. Russell gets to the ball first, but there is no thought of throwing home to try to get Togneri-Jones. It goes straight to the cutoff man to hold Ramirez at second. It doesn't work. He's rounded second and is halfway to third by the time the ball is on the way to the base. He slides, but the play is not close. He would not have gone if it was going to be close. He is too smart to make the last out at third.

The stadium is quiet.

* * *

The playoffs last year were what started the end for Sydney and me. I don't have bad games often, but when I do, I'm not pleasant to be around. I have been known to turn over a cooler, though that was mostly when I was younger. Now, I tend to fume and start shouting matches with anyone who talks to me.

The Championship Series went seven games, and I lost both of mine, including Game Six, which went terribly. I didn't have my control and I gave up a home run at a bad moment. I made it six innings, but I gave up six runs. It was miserable. Sydney wanted to talk afterwards. I don't want to think about it too much. There are times in our lives when we do not acquit ourselves well. That night, I did not acquit myself well. It took a while before I was able to admit it to myself. Dad didn't help. He called because of course he called. It was after a big game. I hadn't done well. He needed to break it down with me. Mostly, he wanted to tell me not to worry about it. "Everybody has days when they don't have it. You didn't have it. Too bad it happened when it did, but nothing to be done."

When I told him I'd had a fight with Sydney he was mad at her. "Doesn't she know anything? You've got to give an athlete time to cool off after something like that. Just shows she doesn't understand."

I don't know what that was. I don't know if he saw his chance to get rid of Sydney and pounced or if he was incapable of being on anyone's side but mine. I don't know, but it started the spiral. Sydney wanted me to apologize. As far as I was concerned, I had nothing to apologize for. There were some overly quiet dinners. Some phone calls where not much was said. We never broke up officially. We just stopped seeing each other. Even this year she came to a few games, but I never told her about any of the stuff that was going on. I was relying on Kristen and Dad for that. I could have used someone to talk to about Sydney, but neither of them were any good for that. Kristen had told me that I was wrong. She wasn't going to change her mind, but she wasn't going to bring it up if I didn't. So I didn't. I mentioned to Dad once that Sydney had come to a game.

"What'd she have to say for herself?"

"She just said she liked watching me pitch."

"Hm."

"What's she supposed to say?"

"Something better than that."

He didn't have anything else to say about it. You'd think he might since he thought she should have more to say.

* * *

The bench is not as silent as the rest of the stadium. We haven't won, but we are aware that the game isn't over. There will be a bottom of the ninth. There is some swearing, some kicking at inanimate objects, some beating of hats against the railing. Coates is up. His at-bat is not as weighty as Ramirez's was, but it is not without significance. What happens here is the difference between needing to score to win and having to score to keep from losing. The game is tied. A tied game in the bottom of the ninth favors us. Let him send a flare to the outfield, though, and the odds swing dramatically. It becomes desperate. We will have to throw everything we have, whatever that means.

But Coates is not Ramirez and he is not Ferris. And this is why hitting someone like him second is folly. Tradition and the book be damned. He is no match for Santiago. He swings and misses. He takes a ball. He watches a strike go by. On the next pitch, Ramon goes way outside. Ramirez or Ferris would never swing at it. But Coates does and looks foolish.

The top of the ninth is over, but not the game. I watch my teammates jog off the field. We're not losing. We're tied. We haven't won, but it is up to us. Manny will be up first. He grabs his bat, but before he goes up to hit, he comes over to me. "Don't worry. It will be fine. Just like I tell you. You won't get the win, but you earn it. They won't take this. We won't let them."

I smile at him and shrug. What else can I do? I am a spectator now and not much more.

Bottom of the Ninth.

Dad was a cranky old man too often, but he loved baseball. I don't know why that's so easy to forget about him. I didn't know anyone who was more fun to watch a good baseball game with. He always complained about bad plays, but he could really get excited about good baseball. I don't think he'd take any issue with tonight's game. We've both played really well. He knows what happened with Ramon is the kind of thing that just happens sometimes. The way I pitched, some of the plays that have been made tonight, Dad would have cheered for those. It wouldn't have mattered which player or which team made them. Dad loved good baseball. He'd have wanted us to have won already, but he'd enjoy the game going to the bottom of the ninth in the way that all baseball fans enjoy such things.

Manny is first up. For his sake, I'm glad we're not behind. We have able hitters on the bench and if we were behind, one of them would be announced in place of Manny. We would do without his defense if it meant staying in the game, but now he is allowed to stride to the plate at least one more time in hopes he might set the table for the more fearsome hitters to follow.

On the mound is Ben Wilson, their version of Ramon. He throws hard and not much else, though he will try to get away with a little change-up every so often. He's not thinking about his change-up against Manny. He's thinking about overpowering him. Strike him out and get one out of the way before he has to handle the real hitters. The first pitch comes in and I see that Manny is still swinging from his heels. He misses badly and falls over. God, Manny, just try to punch it somewhere. Just get on base. Don't try to win it. But there is no reasoning with him. Not now. Wilson starts again. Manny's commitment does not waver. He starts his swing early. So early he has no chance unless he guesses exactly right. I wait for him to fall over again, but instead, there is the familiar crack of wood on leather. It's a loud crack. Much louder than Manny normally manages. I look up at the ball and across the field at the outfielders. The ball is headed toward right-center. They are breaking back hard. Outfielders play Manny shallow, as is wise, but it undoes them here. No one can get to it. It bounces just before the warning track and then off the wall. Manny trots into second base standing. Everyone is screaming and whooping. He claps his hands together and points at me on the bench. I smile and I laugh. What else can I do?

* * *

As much as I might want to blame Dad for what happened with Sydney, it's not like he was there with us. He was only a voice in the back of my head. I didn't have to listen to him. He just wanted me to play well. He knew when I was younger that I got distracted sometimes and didn't play well. If he thought Sydney might be a distraction he wanted her gone. It didn't have anything to do with Sydney or who was right and who was wrong. All that mattered to him was me playing ball.

I'm the one who lost my temper. I'm the one who was stubborn.

* * *

When it comes to games like this, I don't care about any of the things that I see people get worked up about on the internet. It doesn't bother me that I won't get the win. This is fun. Or at least, it will be fun if they can get Manny the rest of the way. He's gotten himself halfway there. All we need is a base hit. He's quick enough. And we have good hitters coming up.

And it sure feels like fun. The crowd will cheer for anyone with the right jersey on right now, but that doesn't mean it isn't nice when you have the right jersey. Sitting on the bench, I can feel the rumble of the crowd through my whole body.

Adam is announced. Adam, who is as good a candidate as anyone to win the game. He gets on base more than anyone else on the team. He starts out by taking ball one, then he swings and misses at a strike. He swings again at the next pitch, but nothing good comes of it. It's a little ground ball to Ramirez who scoops it up and tosses it to first. It doesn't even move the runner. Manny is still standing pat at second base.

* * *

This whole year was strange. Dad kept telling me what to do with Sydney and with Russell, but he was also a lot more willing to talk about the days when I was a kid. Usually, if you brought it up, he'd change the subject or say there was no point in talking about the past. He called me to congratulate me this year when I was named to start the All-Star Game and we talked for a little while. Just the normal kind of reflective stuff, but then he made some offhand comment about how I must be glad I'd practiced so much now, even if I hadn't liked it at the time.

"You never let up. I didn't have a choice."

"You always had a choice."

"I don't think you remember it from my side."

"Did you or did you not stop playing for a year?"

He had a point.

"Do you recall practicing much that year?"

"No."

"There you go."

"But why were you always such a hard ass when I played? You could have been more fun."

"You know I played when I was a kid, right?"

"Of course."

"Just had fun. I didn't get really serious until I was a senior in high school. I was like you, chasin' girls and all that. Except nobody rode me. Senior year my coach asked me why I'd never worked that hard before. I told him I didn't know. He told me I could have been really good if I'd worked that hard. I was already the starting center fielder. I was one of the best players around, but he didn't think I was really good. It got me thinking about what really good was."

"So what? You just wanted me to see how good I could be?"

"That about sums it up."

"What if I didn't want to play baseball?"

"Well, like I said, you always had a choice. But when you were playing, you were mine."

"Out with the sparrows."

"That's right. That was a smart little bit of improvisation on my part."

Whenever you talked to Dad about how he did things, you always ended with how smart he was.

* * *

Matt is up now. Matt is a good hitter, but Ben makes him look like a complete amateur. Baseball is weird like that. Manny isn't doing much more than closing his eyes and swinging as hard as he can and he ends up at second, but Matt is one of the better right fielders in the league and one of the most patient hitters you'll ever see and he strikes out on three pitches. Closers are closers for a reason.

There are two outs now and Manny is still standing at second base. The crowd is restless, but not so loud as they have been. They're getting ready for extra innings. They have a hearty cheer for Russell, who is exactly the player they want up right now. Russell. It just doesn't matter. If you play well, you're a hero. If you play poorly, you're scum. There's no justice.

I sit and watch.

Wilson comes set. When he bats, Russell is as still as a cat preparing to pounce. He does not flinch at the first pitch, which is a ball. He watches it go by. Steps out. Taps his spikes with his bat. Steps back in. Waits. He does not flinch at the second pitch, which is also a ball. He follows the same routine. Everything is routine with Russell and baseball. That is why he is good. He never diverges from the routine. Step out. Tap spikes. Step in. The third pitch is also a ball and the crowd boos. They think Wilson is pitching around Russell. They might be right. Russell is the last batter anyone wants to face in this situation. But Wilson doesn't usually pitch around anyone, and he hasn't been missing by a mile. Sure enough, the next pitch, which Russell again takes, is a strike. A good strike, too. Right on the edge.

The last pitch of the game goes like it would in a movie. If you like, you may imagine it all in slow motion. It will be shown in slow motion until the next game. It is dark. the stadium lights shine. Wilson lifts his knee, comes to the plate. Russell swings. He connects. A line drive shoots off of his bat. A beautiful, arcing line that no fielders have a chance at. It is too high for Ramirez. He doesn't even try. It is too fast for the outfielders, striking the base of the wall in left-center. Manny never has to think about where the ball will land. He hits third and makes the turn without a second thought. Russell runs through the first base bag. There are only two kinds of hits that can end a baseball game. A home run and a single. Doubles and triples are not scored. It is only the run that matters. Manny is the run. The dugout is emptying as he crosses the plate standing. The throw from the outfield is wide, late and pointless. No more than a gesture. I am not a part of the initial crowd. I sit on the bench and stare out at the field. I don't know anything about any of this. Does this mean it matters that I pitched today? We won. We won some because of me and some because of Manny and some because of Russell. Russell will get much of the credit. They will not ask him the questions he was asked at the beginning of the season. He will sign a big contract and no one will ever think about what he was accused of.

So it's hard to move. It's hard to run out and scream and carry on. I can't hug him. I can't pat him on the back. But someone comes and drags me out of the dugout. Tonight, all the good things I do are applauded and all the bad things I do are forgiven. I don't think you get too many days like this. Maybe you get them only when it's too late, for one reason or another, to enjoy them.

When I am out on the field, I smile. Everyone swirls around me. Brian hugs me and Manny hugs me and says, "See, I told you we'd win it." And this makes me cry. Manny feels me weep and he holds on tight and turns me so that I don't face the cameras. "You did good, Zack. You did good," he says. And he holds me and for a few minutes I weep and then I pat him on the back to let him know I am okay. He pulls back and I am sure the cameras are zoomed in on me. I am sure they see that my eyes are still wet. Alex hugs me. Adam hugs me. Carver. Hector. Russell taps me on the shoulder. This is how it is. Brian comes back and puts his arm around me and stands next to me during all the interviews. He deflects questions about Dad and lets me talk about pitching with all the clichés Dad taught me to use. Then it is time to head off the field and down into the clubhouse. As I head down the steps into the dugout, I raise my cap and wave it to the crowd and they cheer loudly. A few minutes later, I hear the same thing just before Russell comes into the clubhouse. I guess I did what they asked me to do.

Postgame.

We lost. There isn't much more to it. It wasn't pretty. I didn't pitch again. Two of the games were close, but that doesn't matter. What matters is that after all that, we lost.

After my game, I stayed in the clubhouse a long time. Brian tried to wait for me, but I told him to go home. I was the last one there. I was just about to go when my phone rang. It was Sydney. I was surprised but I picked up.

"I'm sorry I didn't call until now. I didn't know what to say."

"It's okay."

"You pitched great tonight."

"I was okay."

"You're always too hard on yourself."

"Especially after the bad games."

"I'm sorry about your dad. I liked him."

"I think he liked you, too."

"Zack, tell me if you need anything."

"I will."

This was the best I could do, right then.

Three games later, we were on a plane back home. It's strange to come back to your home city after a playoff loss. Fans are there to greet you. They cheer, but everyone knows that it's kind of weird. That's sports, though. Most of the best teams finish their seasons with a loss. We had a great year, but in the end, we didn't win the World Series.

The stories and commentary that came out ranged from the normal boring stuff to absolutely terrible. One idiot on TV went on and on about how my team should look at me and learn about toughness. Like he was on the mound. Like he has any idea how tough I was or how lucky I was or what any of that has to do with that night.

But it was the falsely sentimental crap that really got to me.

There are some out there who can tell you about what Zack Hiatt went through. There are, no doubt, other athletes who have performed under tragic circumstances. Even others who have performed well while their teammates flailed helplessly around them. Zack Hiatt is not unique. But he is rare.

While we cannot overlook the contributions of Russell Jennings who provided the winning hit in Hiatt's game and was otherwise stunning throughout the series, it is on Hiatt's shoulders that we must lay credit for the lone victory in an otherwise disappointing series.

Pitching only days after the death of his father—a father, it must be noted, who had devoted his life to making his son a big league ballplayer—Hiatt was visibly struggling with his emotions early in his start...

Well, at least they're right about the beginning. They didn't spot the struggles at the end, though. I was having a breakdown, but even now, I think Brian is the only one who has any clue about it. I got out of the inning in impressive fashion, so clearly, I was being tough and not hallucinating.

And then there were the articles that lumped all of the team's "struggles" together. Anyone who compared what I went through to what Russell "went through" assured themselves that they would never get another quote from me. Russell showed toughness, too, they said. Dealing with those accusations. That's all Anne White is now, an accuser.

The fans were pretty bad, too. I got a lot of letters and whatnot thanking me for helping the team. Thanking me for giving them at least one World Series. Saying they hoped I understood how much they appreciate what I did. No, I do not understand because you don't appreciate what I did. You don't know anything. You didn't stand in the snow with my father being lectured about birds. You didn't hear him threaten to beat you with a tire iron. You didn't see him come to every game. You didn't have him as a sounding board whenever something went wrong. You don't understand what it was like to pitch for the first time without him watching. You don't know. Your presumption that you do know disgusts me.

Talk moved to who the team would sign before our uniforms were even clean. Russell and I were both free agents when the World Series ended. He was going to win the MVP, I was a front-runner for the Cy Young. That's a lot of money on the table. The general assumption was that they could afford to keep one of us. I made it easy. I told my agent to find the highest offer he could in a different city and take it. The taste in my mouth was too sour. I didn't want to play in front of these fans any more, even though I knew they were the same as any other set of fans. I didn't want to play with Russell anymore, though he's certainly not the only asshole rapist in the game. I wanted to move on, and so I moved.

During the offseason, I started talking to Mom a lot more. I missed Mom without even knowing it. You call your parents and one of them picks up and you talk and you feel like you've talked to them even if you've talked to only one of them, and if the same one always picks up that phone, you can forget. I forgot about Mom and I shouldn't have. We talked about Dad and we talked about Sydney and we talked about whether I wanted to stay. She made it easier for me to do what I wanted to do. She made it easier for me to apologize even if it didn't matter because I was moving and long distance seemed like too much.

And now, I'm somewhere else. I pitch for a different team. I'm having a good year, but not as good as the last few years. That was bound to happen eventually. You can't get better forever. I still have a while, though. My contract is long and lucrative and I'll do my best to fulfill it. To be good all the way through.

I still think about last year a lot. But it's not so much the World Series I think about the most. It's what came right before. Those months Dad and I started talking about how things were when I was a kid. He had softened a lot. He had told me he was sorry, but one thing lingered. I'd never asked him about it and he'd never brought it up. I think because it hurt both of us.

The night I got us into the Series—the night Dad died—he came down into the clubhouse and stayed for a long time. All the reporters were gone and it was almost time to go home. Dad wasn't leaving until the morning, so he could stay until I left. I waited a little longer than I should have because it felt good to be there with him. There were a few minutes when we were alone in the clubhouse, and I don't know why I picked that moment to ask him about the no-hitter, but I did.

"Why didn't you talk to me after I threw that no-hitter in college?"

I saw his shoulders fall when I said it. He'd been smiling before. He'd looked like a younger man, but now I could imagine what he'd look like when he was older. "You know, Zack, tonight was everything I ever dreamed about when you were a kid."

"I know. We both dreamed about this."

"No, we didn't. I dreamed about it, Zack. You were just a kid when I knew what you had. You dreamed about Christmas. If you dreamed about baseball, it was about meeting your favorite players. You just wanted to have fun."

I looked at him for a minute. I didn't know what to say to this. He was right in his way. I didn't dream about it in an adult way, but I did dream.

Me and Barry Bonds in the backyard. That was a dream. I had dreamed, but they were kid dreams. Dad's were different. Maybe. I'm almost as old now as he was then and I don't know if I dream any differently than when I was small. Maybe the difference is in understanding whether you might be able to have it. I thought about this as I looked at him. I wasn't going to say anything.

"You'd been pitching well the whole time you were in college. You were getting better, too. But when you threw that game... Well, I called. I know you know that. I called you over and over again and then your mom said you were probably out celebrating and that I should let you celebrate."

He stopped again. I think he wanted permission from me to stop talking, but I wanted him to get to the end. I wanted to really hear the answer, so I kept looking at him.

He let out a long sigh before he started up again.

"Your mom was right, I knew she was. I also knew that you didn't need me to coach you anymore. You were going first round. They'd have pitching coaches and trainers wedged so far up your ass you wouldn't be able to think about passing gas without someone asking how your arm felt."

"But you didn't call at all after that."

"What the hell did you want me to do, Zack? You hadn't said three words to me since you left. I didn't know if you were playing because you wanted to or if you were playing to spite me, but I knew you weren't playing to please me. Anything that happened after that was on you. It was your dream from there. It had to be."

It hurt to hear him say all of that because he was right. Looking at it now, with some distance, it was easy to see. When you're a kid, you forget that your parents have feelings. I don't know if it's even forgetting so much as a failure to realize. I'd hurt his feelings. That was all. He didn't call because he was tired of being hurt.

"Tonight was pretty good, though, wasn't it, Dad?"

"Yeah. It was. Tonight was pretty good."

Box Score.

Hitter	AB	R	H	RBI	BB	SO
Ramirez, J SS	3	2	2	2	2	0
Coates, X CF	4	0	0	0	1	4
Ferris, M C	4	0	1	1	0	1
Martin, M RF	3	0	1	1	0	1
Apolinar, M 3B	4	0	0	0	0	1
Takeda, J 1B	4	0	0	0	0	3
Lynch, A LF	4	1	1	0	0	1
Torneri-Jones, A DH	3	1	3	0	1	0
Newhall, J 2B	3	0	0	0	0	0

Hitter	AB	R	H	RBI	BB	SO
Reynolds, A 2B	5	0	2	1	0	0
Lewis, M RF	5	0	0	0	0	2
Jennings, R CF	3	0	2	1	2	0
Gonzalez, A 1B	4	0	0	0	0	0
Rivas, H LF	4	2	3	1	0	1
Snyder, D DH	3	1	1	0	0	0
Woods, B C	4	0	3	1	0	1
Carver, W 3B	4	0	0	0	0	0
Espinosa, M SS	4	2	2	1	0	1

Pitcher	IP	H	R	ER	BB	SO
Guillen, C	5	10	4	4	1	1
St. Onge, J	1	1	0	0	0	1
Ward, F	2	0	0	0	1	2
Wilson, B (L, 0-1)	0.2	2	1	1	0	1

Pitcher	IP	H	R	ER	BB	SO
Hiatt, Z	7	5	2	2	5	7
Lapping-Carr, M	1	0	0	0	0	2
Santiago, R (W, 1-0)	1	3	2	2	0	2

SB - Ramirez

2B - Reynolds 2, Jennings, Rivas 2, Snyder, Espinosa, Ferris

3B - Ramirez

HR - Rivas

SF - Snyder

GIDP - Carver, Ferris, Newhall

Bonus Story: The Catcher.

The aging catcher squats behind the plate receiving warm up pitches from a September call-up thirteen years his junior. This is the last game of the season, and everything hurts. No one on his team knows, but this will be his last game. Only a few people know at all. His wife and parents, an old friend who used to play for his team. Even his children don't know. They are just the right age to unintentionally blab something to a friend or uncle and just like that, the news is everywhere. He doesn't want that.

He has spent the last few years hearing his name mentioned in the same breath as the Hall of Fame. But the mention is perfunctory. Always accompanied by the phrase, "a few more good seasons" or "you have to at least look at him." The kinds of things people say when you fall in that uncomfortable category some refer to as The Hall of Very Good.

He's not complaining, not even mentally. He's not upset by it. He just thinks it's foolish. He has no problem going quietly into the night. He's always been aware of his own limitations. He will not be like so many of those who have come before him and stayed much too long. Scraping every last moment out of the ability they used to possess. Even this year, his worst, he's been respectable. Middling. He's only faded in the last few months.

The bone-on-bone scraping in his knees finally wearing him down.

There is no glory in his last game. His team is out of contention. Bags are already packed. Too many injuries and not enough new blood in the minors to come and fill the holes. They are aging, all of them. His opponents reside on the other side of the spectrum. Bad, yes, but young. Hopeful.

As much as he felt no desire for the farewell tour or the press conference announcing his retirement, he would like to go out with a little flair. A couple of hits. Maybe a homerun. And in contribution to a win. No one wants to lose the last time they take the field. He wants to leave with a skip in his step.

He hopes to coach, maybe even manage. He knows that. He hasn't decided how long he'll take off. Maybe a few years. He'd like to see his children through high school. The idea of not playing—of being home—worries him. He's been playing for more than thirty years. It doesn't matter that he hasn't passed forty. Maybe it even matters more. How many can be so young and honestly claim to have been at the same thing for so long? He loves his wife. He relishes the idea of more time with her, but there are reservations. So many marriages end when the player retires and people who found themselves compatible for a few months at a time find they can't tolerate a full trip around the sun together. It's harder to overlook the little stuff when it's every day. This is what he's heard.

His friend, the one who he has told, is in the stands today. A kind gesture made possible by the pair of cleats that landed on his ankle in the middle of August and ended his season. His friend, Zack, was having a good year, but such things happen and for pitchers, it's better the ankle than the arm. Zack is a truly great player. He's five years younger than the catcher, but already belongs in the Hall of Fame in a way the catcher never will. With a few more years, he might be listed among the all-time greats.

The catcher stares out at the baby sixty feet away and remembers the role he had in molding Zack seven years ago. Already a good pitcher, the catcher brought him the small distance he had left to go. He sees the child before him and knows it's not the same. If it weren't September, and there weren't so many wounded, he would never see a major league mound.

The catcher isn't interested in this kid. He'd rather be catching his friend, but Zack left town after the year they didn't win the series. The catcher remembers the last game they played together. The only game of that Series they won. He wished they had been on the same team the next year, when things broke the right way and the reward they'd all been waiting for materialized. But the catcher understands. In the same circumstance, he might have left, too. Sometimes we have to leave. Zack was never quite the same after he left, but he and the catcher only grew closer. Most believe something broke in Zack when he left. But the catcher doesn't think so. The catcher thinks maybe something was repaired. He'd watch Zack pitch in years after he left and saw that his emotions never overcame him like they had before, not for a moment. He looked like allowed to know a full breath for the first time. The same feeling spread to other parts of his life. He found a woman who was right for him and married her. Soon, they will have a child. Zack is approaching the end of his career and in five or maybe seven years, he will be home all the time. The catcher believes he is just the kind of player who can handle a real home life. Quiet will be good for Zack.

The catcher doesn't want to think about quiet for too long. He wants to move forward. Always forward. He wants to bring others forward with him. He is trying to learn how to do this without hurting too many egos. He can be too strident in his criticism. Other players have been known to bristle under his tutelage.

The game progresses. The call-up throwing to him lasts five innings before he reaches his designated pitch count. He strikes out four and walks three. Two runs score. The catcher is skeptical about the pitcher's potential. There are problems with his delivery. The differences in his pitches show up. But this won't be the catcher's problem. He'll be gone before anyone starts to think about fixing the young man out there.

He's decided to announce his retirement at Christmas so that he might be a footnote rather than the story of the day. He imagines fans half-comatose from Christmas dinner, scrolling absent-mindedly on their phones and commenting to someone briefly, "Guess who retired?" and then getting on with their holiday.

At bat, he's not having the day he wanted to have. He's struck out twice and hit a weak ground-er back to the pitcher. His bat is slow now, this is only natural. Everything about him is slow. He is able to survive on guile. He can guess right better than half the time, and until recently, that's been more than enough. So many of the pitchers he faces at this time of year are new. That's made it harder on him, that lack of history. This time, his last at bat, he's facing a reliever he's seen many times before. The catcher takes two off pitches to make sure he knows what's coming next, and then he sends a sharp little single past the second baseman and into right centerfield. It's the eighth inning. He knows it will be the last at-bat of his career and, for a moment, he considers asking for the ball. But that might tip his hand. He watches it return to the mound and then he watches the next batter foul it off into the stands with the very next pitch.

He finishes with a single, but that's all. Those batting behind him don't manage to move him along. The inning ends and, shortly thereafter, the game. His team wins five to three. He likes that he goes out on a win. That he finished his career with a hit. Even in a meaningless game, those things carry some meaning for him.

He doesn't linger in the clubhouse. That's not his way. Zack comes into the clubhouse, and winds his way among the few people he still knows. The catcher watches his friend gingerly make his way across the room.

The catcher looks up. "No crutches. Are you finally toughening up?"

"Nah," Zack says, "I'd still be in bed if they let me. But it seems the men who sign my checks think I should rehab."

"Well, as long as it's not toughness."

"That's not something you have to worry about. I'm soft to the core."

They talk for a few minutes as the catcher, performing his last duties as a player, straightens his locker and cleans out his things. Then they walk out together. The pitcher and the man who used to catch him.

Acknowledgments

Before the new version of The Hardball Times launched, Dave Studenmund had already committed to publishing all of this novel, and it wasn't nearly finished yet. So first, I would like to thank Studes for his faith in making that commitment.

I would also like to thank Paul Swydan, David Appelman and Joe Distelheim for their roles in publishing this novel, Brooke Howell for her fantastic illustrations and Travis Howell for the cover. Thanks also to *Cincinnati Enquirer* beat reporter C. Trent Rosecrans for a bit of clubhouse insight.

Finally, I would like to thank my wife, Cate Linden, who is my first and best reader. As a writer, nothing is more valuable than having a spouse who also writes and who cares enough to tell you when you stink. Everything I write would be worse were it not for her.

21014237R00128

Made in the USA
San Bernardino, CA
02 May 2015